Heartbreak Gone Good

BY CHENIER DATILUS

DORRANCE PUBLISHING CO
EST. 1920
PITTSBURGH, PENNSYLVANIA 15238

Dorrance Publishing Co
585 Alpha Drive
Pittsburgh, PA 15238
Visit our website at *www.dorrancebookstore.com*

ISBN: 978-1-6491-3100-3
eISBN: 978-1-6480-4557-8

Heartbreak Gone Good

CHARLIE ARRIVED THE FIRST DAY OF WORK ON A COLD OVERCAST morning wearing a light gray pinstripe suit, white cotton shirt, dark blue necktie, and a newly procured black briefcase. He smelled of freshly splashed aftershave and walked assertively through the front entrance of the lobby with all the optimism of a proven winner. As soon as Charlie entered the building's massive lobby, however, his confidence swiftly gave way to apprehension as he felt lost in a labyrinth of hidden hallways, stairs, exits, and a dizzying number of patrons coming and going in different directions. Fortunately for Charlie, one of the building's security guards, a chubby, middle-aged Black woman, noticed his uneasiness and waved him over.

"Who are you here to see, young man?" she asked in a patient, gentle tone.

Her gray hair was pulled back in a severe tight bun, and her makeup was tastefully done. She had the right amount of lipstick and eye shadow. From the way she wore her uniform—clean, pressed, organized, not a button out of place or trace of lint— Charlie sensed she was a proud woman, a woman of integrity, a woman with strong personal and professional pride who took her employment seriously. He studied her for a while longer, then opened his briefcase and searched for the contact's name at the firm. He finally located her scribbled name at the bottom of a blank page written in black ink.

"I'm here to see Julie Warner at Weiss, Paul & Ginsburg. She's expecting me."

"Okay honey, let me see your picture ID."

Charlie handed over his driver's license and the security guard—Norma was the name attached to her name tag—placed a call to Weiss, Paul & Ginsburg's mainline.

Moments later Norma announced, "Mr. Black has arrived; he's here to see Ms. Warner."

He only heard her side of the conversation but gathered everything was okay by her nodding and her sweet smile in his direction. She placed the phone down, handed Charlie back his ID, and spoke calmly into her walkie-talkie, "He's good to go. Jeff, please escort him to the second bank of elevators and key him to the thirty-second floor."

Weiss, Paul & Ginsburg LLP was a world-renowned legal powerhouse with thirty office locations in the United States, Europe, and Asia. From its very outset, the firm shook up the legal profession: rewriting the rules for success, and in the process, displacing the venerable institutions that considered their place atop the legal food chain a divine right. As a practice, the firm only took on the most complex and high-profile business litigation and corporate mergers and acquisition matters on behalf of the world's largest corporations, banks, and political institutions. And to contend with the Cravath, Swaine & Moores of the worlds, Weiss, Paul & Ginsburg hired the very best and brightest the Ivy League schools had to offer and then weaponized them against the opposition. Mr. Weiss, the late founding partner's motto for clients was, "You hire us to get results. Nothing else matters."

Over time the firm's lore became the stuff of legends and the once three attorney firm grew exponentially, expanding to over 1,400 attorneys in a sixty-year span. Weiss, Paul &

Ginsburg expanded internationally to account for its global clients, opening up offices in prominent locations, such as London, Hong Kong, Paris, Madrid, Shanghai, and Tokyo. Office headquarters was located in the heart of the financial district in downtown Los Angeles, where an army of attorneys and support staff worked seemingly around the clock.

The firm's leadership was run by a management committee of five partners, but the true reins of power resided with one man: Michael Patterson. Mr. Patterson had a robust client roster of large banks, investment firms, and fortune 500 companies. He was on first name basis with powerful CEOs, investment bankers, judges, and politicians across the political spectrum. He was a very complex and brooding man, known for his explosive fits of rage and belittling condescension. Mr. Patterson was also known to bully and terrorize staff, associates, and partners alike. No one was spared from his volcanic temper.

The scuttlebutt was that one day a lowly office services clerk casually called Mr. Patterson "Michael" while delivering his mail. It took a United Nations-like intervention to keep Mr. Patterson from firing the poor clerk. Several partners and senior human resources personnel literally begged Mr. Patterson for leniency before he decided to let the clerk off with a stern warning and one day of docked pay. Years later the story was still shared with all newcomers, a stern reminder of the potential perils of crossing paths with Mr. Patterson. Though not particularly fond of ageless rumors, Charlie nonetheless appreciated the information as he figured knowing the pitfalls ahead of time was better than not knowing anything at all.

When Charlie reached the thirty-second floor, he quickly exited the elevator and headed to reception. Once there he was captivated by the exquisite décor: sparkling dark hardwood floors led the path, a Givenchy Royal Hanover Chandelier offered elegant lighting, and rare Rembrandt paintings epitomized the measure of the firm's great wealth. The reception desk featured a sophisticated single curved end, combining a floating glass, silver accents, and rich mahogany laminate, which was eye-catching, yet functional. Upon arriving at the reception desk, he calmly introduced himself. The receptionist, a petite, young Hispanic woman with jet black hair, welcomed his arrival with a gracious smile, displaying a perfect set of straight, gleaming white teeth. Her nails were meticulously manicured, each finger coated in bright red polish. She wore a well-tailored pencil skirt, a white blouse, and dark blazer. Her skin was radiantly flawless; it looked as if it had been kissed by the sun.

"Hi, Mr. Black, nice to meet you. My name is Cecilies Rodriguez, but you can call me Cece. Easier to remember, and it saves me the hassle of having to correct people on the proper pronunciation of my name," she said with a half-smile.

Cece spoke with supreme confidence, in a rapid and clipped manner, pronouncing each word crisply and intelligently. She moved around the edge of her desk, walked over to where Charlie was standing, and they exchanged handshakes. In the interlude, three telephone lines sprung to life. Cece picked up the cradle, "Weiss, Paul & Ginsburg, please hold." She repeated the process with each call before returning to the original caller, "Thank you for holding; how may I help you? Mr. Ginsler is in pre-trial conference; would you like his voicemail? I'll patch you through. Have a nice day."

After she cleared the phone lines of the remaining calls, Cece turned her attention to Charlie and said, "Charlie, Ms. Julie Warner, head of human resources, knows you are here and will be with you in a moment. Please have a seat. While you wait for Ms. Warner, may I offer you some refreshments. Would you like some tea, coffee, or water?"

"Some water would be nice. Thank you."

CECE NODDED CHARLIE'S WAY, PRESSED THE INTERCOM, AND said to someone in office services, "Please send a bottle of water to reception."

Moments later the bottle water was delivered to Charlie's table. In his nervous excitement, Charlie neglected to take a sip of the water before Julie strolled in with a large grin on her face. Julie was tall, athletically lean, and graceful. Each step she took felt like a warm Caribbean breeze in the still of the night. Freckles dotted a pale but glowing face, and she had an arresting head of red locks with streaks of gray lightly peppered throughout. Julie was impeccably attired in a gray blazer over a black jumpsuit with black pumps and light jewelry. She had on perfume, but the summery scent wasn't terribly overbearing.

"Charlie, nice to see you made it here okay. How are you?"

"Just fine. Pleased to be here and ready to get started."

"Well of course you are. But before we throw you to the wolves—pardon the expression, but I've always liked that phrase—we have some housekeeping to attend to. Follow me to the back office where you'll need to complete required paperwork. Fun stuff like medical benefits, 401k, employee handbook, etcetera. You know, fun stuff," Julie said without a hint of sarcasm.

"When you're done with that, someone from office services will get you set up with your employee ID and parking card. First things first, let's get through the paperwork. Then I'll take you on a firm-wide tour and will introduce you to some key folks whom you'll be working with day-to-day."

A few minutes later, Julie guided Charlie to a non-descript, windowless office and left him to his business.

"Have Cece page me when you're done here," uttered Julie before leaving the room.

Assessing the paperwork, Charlie quickly scanned through the thick employee manual, signed a few confidentiality agreements promising the firm his soul and first born, and then waded through a packet of other standard employee benefit documents: 401k, medical, dental, disability, short and long-term life insurance. With that accomplished, Charlie stood up to stretch out his stiff legs and back. He checked his watch and gathered he had spent forty-five minutes of his life he'd never get back on administrative paperwork. He circled back to reception and had Cece page Julie.

"Welcome back from the living dead…I told you this paperwork stuff was fun," Julie quipped.

Charlie didn't know what to make of Julie's light-hearted comments, so he remained silent.

Julie continued, "Now that you're done with the paperwork, I'd like to introduce you to a few of your co-workers."

With Julie leading the way, Charlie met a staggering number of people from various departments and hierarchy. Despite being overwhelmed by the considerable volume of individuals he met and the vast amount of information thrusted upon him, Charlie keenly remembered Brandy Smith, a lovely lady with a reassuring smile and easy demeanor. After thirty years at the firm, twenty as records manager, she was on the retirement trail. Charlie wondered if that was the reason for her uncontrolled excitement. She pumped his hand with such force and delight that his left shoulder felt out of socket. After Julie rounded out her excursion of most of the office services staff, she had Charlie visit the attorneys.

The partners' offices were luxuriously decorated with large plush sofas, mahogany desks, oil paintings, and panoramic views of the city's skyline. The associates, bless their souls, had more modest work rooms. Instead of the large picturesque rooms more typically illustrated in Architectural Digest, they hunkered in small, cramped, windowless rooms. As with all major multi-national law practices, partnership status had to be earned and the Weiss way was to squeeze every ounce of blood, sweat, and tears from their foot soldiers.

"Oh, by the way, I left an introduction out, but he's very important to our process." "Who's that?" Charlie asked quizzically.

"This way; we're heading back to office services to meet Joe Pascal. He's the manager of office services, been with our illustrious firm for twenty years. You need something, go to Joe. The guy can almost do anything. The partners love the guy, he's saved their skins dozens of times. No matter how trying the circumstances or how tight the deadline, Joe seems to always get it done. To date the firm has never missed a court or client deadline with Joe at the helm. He runs a well-oiled machine."

When Julie and Charlie reached office services' main hub, they walked past a horde of people intensely busy at work. Everyone appeared laser focused at their task, and the sheer number of documents being photocopied and scanned was staggering.

"Charlie, meet Joe," Julie motioned.

Joe shook Charlie's hand, patted him firmly on the back, and uttered, "You'll get to know me better than anyone else in here. We're the firm's lifeblood." To keep Julie from hearing what he had to say, Joe pulled Charlie aside and said in a low voice, "I'll also give you the low down, like whom to avoid. There are some dangerous snakes here that can make your life very miserable."

Charlie nodded his head appreciatively but said nothing. He wasn't sure what to think, but insider scoop was always helpful.

"Ahem," Julie cleared her throat, "Hope you two enjoyed your private bro moment, but I have a busy schedule of meetings to attend to, so we have to keep this locomotive moving."

Before she did, however, Julie went over to Joe and said in a cold tone, "I hope you're not doing anything untoward and creating unnecessary issues by putting things in his mind he won't be able to flush out."

"I wouldn't dare do such a thing, Julie."

"That's Ms. Warner to you; you'll address me properly. The partners here think you walk on water, but I'm not of that ilk. Be careful, Joe. Every superman has his kryptonite." With that, Julie turned away, signaled to a bewildered Charlie to follow, and left the normally loquacious Joe stone quiet.

After her little kerfuffle with Joe, Julie walked past a few senior associate offices. She nodded in the direction of Janet Wong, a six-year Yale Law School alumna and rising star, and Hamir Besed, a summa cum laude graduate of NYU Law School and former Supreme Court Clerk who was up for a partnership vote in the coming weeks.

"Do these people ever leave their offices?" Charlie asked uneasily.

"Of course, to use the bathroom and sleep."

Observing Charlie's bemused expression, Julie added, "That's a joke, Charlie. Of course, they leave their offices. Everyone works hard here, but people take their vacations, too. I am sure you're aware of the firm's generous vacation policy by now. Two weeks away after five years of employment, three weeks for six to ten years of service, and a month of vacation after ten years. You throw in the major holidays and watch out; you're talking Club Med here. Anyway, to finish our tour, let's head over to Mr. Patterson's office. He is our esteemed partner and head of the revered management committee."

Mr. Patterson's corner office came with its own receptionist, a senior secretary, an executive assistant, and a senior paralegal.

At 1,000 square feet, the extravagant office was larger than most Los Angeles apartments. It was outfitted with a lustrous dark mahogany desk, plush leather chairs, a well-kept beige sofa, a private bathroom, kitchenette, and a hefty bookshelf with rows of legal books.

"The man simply runs the firm," Julie stated.

"So I've been told," Charlie replied.

"What else have you been told about him?" Julie quizzed.

"That people fear him. That the sun rises and sets on him."

"That's a bit hyperbolic, isn't it?" Julie said with a questioning stare. "The part about people fearing him may be overblown. He has the respect of the partners and the staff alike, that's all."

Charlie had a feeling Julie was toeing the company line, but he didn't dare challenge her statement.

"I believe we've had enough for today. I've given you a rough layout of where things are, but you obviously will need to spend time on your own to get more acquainted with the place. The person whom you'll work most closely with, however, is your paralegal manager, Sherrie Mason."

Heaven and earth moved the moment Charlie laid eyes on Sherrie—she was remarkable.

Sherrie cut an alluring figure with athletic lean arms, long, shapely, tanned legs, luscious big lips, piercing blue eyes the color of the ocean, and strawberry blond hair, which flowed nimbly down her shoulders. She dazzled in a fitted navy-blue blazer and skirt that accentuated her extraordinary curves. She wore a red sash belt for a hint of color, black pumps, silver necklace, and a bangle on each arm. She walked with purposeful strides and a glint of seductiveness that was unforgettable: Sherrie owned the space.

"I'm told you're Charlie Black, the newbie paralegal on our

team. Welcome." Sherrie patted Charlie on his right shoulder but did not extend her hand for a customary handshake. She sized Charlie up and smiled expressively. "I'm the famous or infamous Sherrie Mason," she uttered, "It really depends on who's telling the story. Now, darling, I don't lose much sleep over it because envy is the root of all ambition. But enough about that, I didn't come here to gossip. Lord knows there's enough of that going around in this place. I don't need to add to the ledger."

Sherrie moved in a few inches closer to Charlie and said, "Let me tell you how it is here. I set the pace, come up with legal strategy, and do whatever it takes to make sure Michael looks good. That's Michael Patterson, our rain making partner, if you don't already know."

"Yes, Julie and a few others briefed me on Mr. Patterson's reputation."

"Well then you already know what's at stake. Good for you. Ahead of the curve already, I see. I think you'll do just fine here, as long as you follow my explicit orders." Sherrie ignited Charlie's passion. He couldn't shake his overwhelming desire to caress her lips, arms, or any part of her that would satisfy his perilous urges for her. Thankfully Sherrie interrupted his thoughts, "I have a meeting to prepare for, and I expect you there. Michael will need all hands-on deck."

Charlie quickly regained his focus, hoping his inner thoughts weren't obvious to those around him, and asked, "What time is the meeting?"

"12:00 P.M. sharp. Oh, Charlie, I can't stress this enough. Michael doesn't tolerate tardiness, and neither do I. The meeting is in the Kennedy Conference room; it's adjacent to the office services department."

Before he could soak it all in, Charlie heard Sherrie's

footsteps down the hall as she made her way to the elevator. *Important footsteps*, he thought.

At a quarter to 12:00 P.M., hordes of lifeless souls piled into the Kennedy Conference Room, their faces masked in scowls. The Kennedy Conference Room was the largest of seven conference rooms with a few decorative touches of abstract paintings and other nondescript artwork on the wall to manufacture warmth. By the time Charlie entered the room, he noticed all the back seats were taken and found a seat near the front across from a young woman with dark brown hair and an oval face. Her head was lowered, and she pretended to be preoccupied with her notes. She scribbled a few unintelligible things on her notepad and never looked up. Several of her colleagues were of the same mindset; the conference room was a sea of bowed heads and bored faces. On occasion a few of the meeting attendees punched keys on their cell phones and engaged in idle chatter, but that was the extent of their brazenness.

Charlie stared straight ahead and mused to himself, *What a miserable scene.*

He lightly tapped his fingers on the wood table to relieve his mounting tension. The scene inside the conference room was tortuous, like attending an execution with no idea whose head was next on the chopping block. Finally, at 12 P.M. sharp, Mr. Patterson arrived abruptly with Sherrie in tow.

When Mr. Patterson entered the room, everyone snapped to rapt attention. The room became uncomfortably quiet and still. All sidebar conversations ceased. Writing on notepads and texting on cellphones also ended. One could hear a pin drop. Without a wasted moment, Mr. Patterson barreled his way to the front of the room, slammed his well-worn brown briefcase on the table and peered directly at the sea of mourners.

By the way he entered the room, one could tell Mr. Patterson was a bit of a showman. He seemingly enjoyed the attention and respect someone of his stature commanded, and the power he wielded over his subordinates was unquestionably intoxicating to him. In the looks department, he was far from handsome. Mr. Patterson looked like the American actor Fyvush Finkel but was considerably pudgier with unflattering bulges in areas you wouldn't expect. His hair was short, wavy, and regal silver, and his face sported a perpetual five o'clock shadow. Mr. Patterson's suit was meticulously tailored, however, fitting his large frame seamlessly.

He wasted no time getting down to business. "<u>Knapp v. Edison Pharmaceuticals</u> is a major case for our firm with significant implications for our client," he bellowed as he paused to examine the room, ensuring he had everyone's undivided attention.

No one seemed to blink, or breathe for that matter. They hung on his every word as if spellbound.

He continued, "For those of you who are unfamiliar with this case, I'm going to provide a brief refresher, so listen carefully. I will not repeat myself nor will I entertain silly questions. Edison Pharmaceuticals, our new client, has requested a substitution of counsel because previous counsel was absurdly incompetent in handling their case. Quite frankly, some of those attorneys should be disbarred for gross negligence, but that's neither here nor there. Edison came to us to change the trajectory of this case, to perform miracles—and miracles we intend to perform. Ever since John Knapp and his group of attorneys brought this wrongful death lawsuit against our client, arguing Edison's heart medication led to his son's death, the case has taken a life of its own. Thousands of other plaintiffs have made similar claims, so we have our work cut out for us. However, with a $10 million retainer on the line, we have plenty of motivation to knock this out of the park."

Patterson paused momentarily and looked toward the back of the room before turning his attention to his chief paralegal, "Sherrie, I'll need you to quickly file a notice of substitution of counsel and continuance with Judge Pete Seton, so we can adequately prepare for the upcoming trial." Returning his focus back on the group, Mr. Patterson said, "I don't need to remind any of you the importance of this case for our client. We don't lose, nor will we tolerate a loser's mentality here. Do I make myself clear?"

"Yes, Mr. Patterson," everyone said in unison.

"Fantastic," he said, "Sherrie Mason will be the head paralegal on this case. She will run the trial team, handle trial preparation, and designate work assignments for the junior paralegals and support staff."

Before Michael could articulate another word, Sherrie interjected, "I run a tight ship, and I don't accept shoddy work product or excuses. I demand and expect perfection. We work to win. Nothing else matters. Is that sufficiently clear?"

Everyone nodded in agreement. Michael smiled approvingly and whispered something inaudible in Sherrie's left ear. She laughed openly before quickly turning her attention back to the assembly.

She announced, "Meeting adjourned. I'll be by shortly with everyone's individual work assignments."

Once the group shuffled out of the conference room, Charlie headed back to his workstation. When Charlie finally reached his small corner cubicle, he took inventory of his work area. He was underwhelmed by the drab appearance, but nonetheless he was relieved to finally be alone. Warming up to his situation, he took stock of his large gray desk and money tree—an appropriate symbolism of what the law firm seems to value most: wealth and money.

Recognizing his office space wasn't up to his standards, Charlie searched for a cleaning spray and dry cloth to wipe the area clean and found them in the bottom drawer of his desk. With a little elbow grease, he rid his desk of dust and other particles. He encountered less hassle cleaning the computer; it was considerably less grimy, and he was able to sanitize everything in short order. Eager to get started, Charlie pressed the computer's start button, waited for the dinosaur to boot, and then inputted the visible password left on his desk. He then set up his email and handled a few routine tasks with instructions carefully laid out for him. Done with those tasks, he turned his attention to organizing his work area. Charlie placed the human resources policy handbook, health benefits info, and office map into a manila folder he pulled out from one of his desks drawers and labeled it "On Boarding Documents." Afterwards he rubber-banded together pens, pencils, highlighters, markers and placed those items in a blue ceramic cup on his desk.

Just as he was finished, Sherrie walked in. She had two red well folders in her hands. Charlie raced over to help her unload.

"I've heard great things about you, and I'm sure the sentiments are all true. I know you haven't had much of a chance to settle in with the pace being so frantic, but it is probably for the best. We want to indoctrinate you in our way of doing things. You see, Charlie, this isn't an ordinary firm; this is a magical place. Whatever you're thinking about accomplishing, think bigger."

Seizing on the fact Charlie was hanging on her every word, Sherrie grabbed a chair from a nearby cubicle and sat directly across from him. She crossed and uncrossed her legs a few times, which caused her skirt to slowly ride up her thighs. And her slightly unbuttoned shirt showed just enough cleavage to grab Charlie's attention. Sherrie, with her sexuality on display, watched Charlie expectantly, anticipating what his reaction might be. Charlie tried valiantly to avert his eyes, but the trap was set. She had him. He knew it and she knew it, too.

Sherrie observed as Charlie stirred uncomfortably in his chair, watched him touch his chin, scratch his forehead, crack his knuckles. She watched him do everything he could to avoid staring at her, and she enjoyed every minute of his discomfort. Like a fly stuck in a spider's web, the more Charlie fought to extricate himself from her allure, the more entangled he became. Without saying a word, Sherrie removed a collection of documents from the folder and handed it to him.

"I've taken the liberty of creating a worksheet that lays out your assignments for the Edison matter. You'll have other projects, but this one is paramount. In billing alone, Michael stands to generate over $25 million dollars in legal fees for the firm."

"Wow, that's quite impressive."

"Oh, Charlie, it's a lot more than that. But let's not get ahead of ourselves with the applause. First, I need you to familiarize yourself with the crux of this case: the plaintiff's position, the underlying issues, the judge's rulings on prior counsel's motions, our defense strategy, and other pertinent issues critical to this matter."

"I can handle that. Do you need a write-up on it?"

"I don't need any more work on my plate. Just let me know your thoughts after reviewing the files. We can discuss it over lunch. I imagine you're starved."

"That I am. What do you have in mind?"

"Great, I know just the place."

Sherrie drove Charlie along Chester Ave in her new BMW convertible until they arrived at Café Bohemian, a quaint two-story American eatery renowned for its appetizing delicacies and eclectic patrons. By the time they reached Café Bohemian's front steps at a quarter to 2:00 P.M., a late lunch by all measures, the normally raucous crowd had all but petered out, except for a few stragglers. Sherrie secured a corner table near a window where the shade was drawn for privacy.

When the skinny waitress looked in Sherrie's direction, she said, "One Mojito and Cosmopolitan," handing the menu ceremoniously to Charlie with a smile and stated, "The burgers are fantastic here"—and to the waitress— "I'll have a grilled chicken on rye with a side salad."

"And for you, sir?" the waitress asked.

"I'll do a burger, medium well, with fries."

When the waitress returned with their drinks, Sherrie picked up the Mojito and handed it to Charlie, "You need this, darling."

He accepted the drink, looked at Sherrie, and in a lowered voice uttered, "Here's to our future success."

Sherrie smiled at him playfully and sipped her Cosmopolitan. She could see in Charlie's face he was debating whether to sip his drink slowly or down it all at once as if it were no big deal. Noticing his indecision, she said, "You may want to take it in slowly if you want to avoid being tipsy at work."

Heeding her advice, Charlie tasted it delicately and then set his drink down.

Ensuring his attention was still on her, Sherrie lightly touched the top of Charlie's right hand and said, "So, darling, what's your story?"

"I'm embarrassed to say I don't have one."

"Oh, off with the modesty; everyone has a story."

"I am just an average Joe from the Midwest—"

"Or there you go again. Don't bore me with this average Joe stuff. Talk to me, Charlie. I'm all ears," Sherrie said, shifting slightly in her seat.

"Look, I am not used to talking about myself. I, I—"

"Nonsense. We all like to talk about ourselves, darling. Don't you know humans are narcissistic creatures by nature? Give the quietest person you know a chance to talk about his or herself, and you may never get that person to shut up."

Charlie snickered, "I guess I can't get out of answering this question, can I?"

"You guessed right."

"Okay, now that you've beaten it out of me, I'm one of three kids and a certified momma's boy."

"I wouldn't say that too loudly if you want to attract the opposite sex. Momma's boys are low on the list of desirable mates, darling."

"I am sure you are right, but I stand by my statement. My mom was like a momma bear. She would do anything for her family, and I adored that part about her the most. Mom had a gorgeous head of hair before chemo stripped her of it."

"Oh my, a woman's hair is everything to her. Losing her hair like that must have been terribly depressing for her."

"It was. She started losing small amount of hair strands at first and then large chunks of hair came out all at once. Being a person who took pride in her appearance, it hurt my mom deeply to watch her hair disintegrate before her eyes. But she was brave and she did her best to shield her agony from her friends and family. She wore lots of wigs; she felt they kept people from asking too many questions about her appearance and diagnosis."

Charlie was now fidgeting in his seat. The memory of those dark days troubled him, and he worried of his emotions bubbling over.

"I'm sorry, Charlie. I can't imagine the anguish she must have felt," Sherrie sympathetically grabbed his right hand and rubbed it softly, "Thank you for sharing this with me about your mom. Makes me feel closer to you already."

Bringing her hand back to her drink, Sherrie whirled her Cosmopolitan around and said, "I suspect the wigs at some point made her feel alive again and offered your mom a degree of humanity and pride."

"I suppose," Charlie said agreeably.

While Charlie was talking, the waitress arrived with their food. Sherrie picked up her grilled chicken sandwich, took a bite and said, "Charlie, your burger is getting cold."

"I suppose I'm not that hungry after all."

"But you must eat something," She grabbed the steak knife on Charlie's side and proceeded to cut his burger in two even pieces and handed one to him. "It will do you some good. You'll thank me later; today is going to be a late night at the office."

He took the offering from Sherrie, took a sizable first bite, and chewed his remaining burger until nothing was left.

"It was very good," he chimed cheerfully. "The meat was exquisitely tender. My compliments to the cook!"

"That's the spirit, now tell me about your dad."

Charlie sighed, "Even though my dad could barely make ends meet, he wanted Mom to be a homemaker and raise the kids. But Mom wouldn't hear of it. She wanted to work, to make her own money. After her relentless campaign for independence, he eventually caved. She got her first and only job at a small consumer products manufacturing plant just a few miles north of our house. The factory produced lotions and hand soaps for wholesale retailers and department stores. She was in her early thirties when she started working at the factory, worked there nearly thirty years. The long hours and monotony would sometimes wear on her, but she was unrelenting in her endeavor to earn her own money. Mom showed up to work nearly every day during her tenure. I don't know how she managed it with three growing needy kids and an almost useless husband, but she did."

"Independence, my dear. Every woman yearns to have control over her own life and destiny, pride of knowing you can do for yourself. An admirable trait if you ask me."

"That must have been it," Charlie said, "With her own money, she had the freedom to buy her own clothes without having to nag my dad, Paul, for money. She was comforted knowing she could always buy her kids new toys during the holidays instead of taking in hand me downs from her parents, which she viewed as degrading. It was important for her to demonstrate to herself and her family that she did not need a man to take care of her and her children. Having said that, Mom had a roguish side to her as well."

"Oh," Sherrie said, "Do tell."

"My innocent mother, at least that's how I have always envisioned her, would routinely bring home some of the factory's products. What appeared a trivial hobby morphed into something more elaborate. In no time, she had amassed shelves of lotions and soaps, which she would diligently repackage and assemble in a room she turned into a makeshift boutique. Before long Mom established a very lucrative side business, selling the products to friends, neighbors, and family members for a sizeable profit."

"How remarkable she had the ingenuity to turn it into a lucrative business! Is that where you get your smarts, from your mom?"

"I suppose," Charlie beamed proudly.

"What was your dad like? You barely mentioned him this entire time. Did you two not get along?"

"Well, as an adolescent, I did not care much for him. He had so much talent, but to be honest with you, he was just too darn lazy and impulsive to make good use of them. Dad was chronically unemployed; a salesman one day, a laborer the next, and a carpenter after that. The list of occupations he held was too long to keep count. He was too impatient to be good at any of his jobs, and he never lasted. If a co-worker, supervisor, or just about anyone spoke to him in a way he did not like, he was out the door, his family responsibilities be damned. In between looking for and being fired from various jobs, my dad played the lotto several times a week, hoping for the big score, but it never materialized. This resulted in Mom often being the sole bread winner for our family."

"How shameful."

"Drove my mom, Elena, crazy and led to numerous bitter arguments. I hated him for a long time, but I learned to understand him better later in life."

"How so?"

"I originally believed Dad was cold, distant, selfish, and indifferent to his family's needs, that he considered his kids as inconveniences, little mistakes who destroyed his lifelong dreams and kept him from realizing things he wanted for himself. I thought that maybe he was ashamed of us and settled for Mom and the monotonous life parenting and husband offered. I know better now. Dad did the best he could and provided us a decent home life. Like many families, we had family gatherings and holiday parties and got a handful of toys for Christmas. It wasn't much, but for the most part, we were happy. Deep down I knew he cared a lot about us, but Dad never showed it like Mom."

"But he showed it in his own way," Sherrie added.

"Yes," Charlie chimed in. "In retrospect I can't blame him now. Dad wanted more from his life. He was an individual, too, not just a father and a husband. His impatience and his desire to become more and his get rich quick attempts were a result of Dad wanting to be great, not just for himself but for all of us. Looking back on it now, he simply wanted my mom and us to be proud of him. His failure as a provider must have slowly eroded his confidence and sense of self. After Dad passed away from complications due to diabetes, Mom died a year later. I wholeheartedly believe she died of a broken heart and not from cancer. How does one cope with life when your soulmate leaves you behind? How does one deal with that? Dad was the only man Mom had known romantically, he was her best friend and life partner," Charlie paused and then uttered, "I am sharing too much."

"Nonsense. We're bonding. We're going to get to know a lot about each other working together, so we might as well start now."

"Seriously I've blabbered too much. What about you, Sherrie? What was your upbringing like?"

"Putting me on the spot, aren't you?"

"Yes, I am," Charlie said. "Unless we are out of time; I know we have to get back to work."

"I am the clock, and we go back when I say it's time," Sherrie said as she continued. "My upbringing doesn't quite have the flair of my reputation, but we all must start from somewhere. I grew up in a solid middle-class family of five. I'm the youngest of three siblings. My brother and twin sister still reside on the northside of Chicago, the same block where we were raised. Talk about boring. Ugh, I'd rather jump off a bridge. Anyhow my mom and dad are proprietors of a very successful brewery, which they inherited from my paternal grandfather. The brewery is a fixture in the local community; it has been around since the early seventies. My grandfather, God bless him, was a man with strong convictions and believed hard work was the answer to all prayers."

"Amen to that," Charlie said.

Sherrie eyed Charlie curiously. She eased in a smile, then circled back to her earlier thought, "Though successful his style was a bit grating. He never learned to relax. As they say, all work and no play makes for a dull boy. Well, my grandfather was immensely dull. All business, all the time," Sherrie said as she stifled a yarn. "Shortly before he passed, my grandfather handed the torch to my father, Jim. Told him some cornball stuff like, 'I'm giving you the opportunity of a lifetime, son. Now that it's yours, make me proud.' "My dad never looked back, and the brewery has been growing ever since."

"What's the name of the brewery?"

"The Brewery House. I know, the name is far from original, but I did not come up with it. I certainly wouldn't have named it that if it had been my choice."

"What would you have named it if it were your choice?" Charlie asked casually.

"Not that," Sherrie said in a slightly annoyed tone. "Oh, Charlie, you have to keep the interruptions to a minimum. I don't have all day. Anyway, getting back to my story, the Brewery House recently added two new locations: one in downtown Chicago, and the other location in a gentrified area of Detroit where they've taken advantage of the renaissance in that city. People used to run away from Detroit, now everybody wants a piece of the action."

"People are flocking to Detroit? I thought all the residents moved out," Charlie said mockingly.

"Not all," Sherrie said with a slight irritation in her voice and continued, "Sales exceeded the $5 million mark the past five years, and demand for good beer has exceeded supply. Grandpa found the magic formula when he started the brewery in his basement. I worked at the brewery on and off during college, and the plan my father had for me and my siblings was to take over the family business when my parents retired. But I scuttled those plans when I left Chicago to pursue a law career. The thought of working the family business for the rest of my life sounded like a death sentence. I couldn't runaway fast enough."

"I imagine your parents were disappointed."

"Yes, Dad was furious and vowed to cut me out of his will, but Mom understood. That was his dream, not mine. Besides, I am an independent woman who beats to her own rhythm. I don't appreciate people planning my life for me. I prefer to be the one writing, directing, and starring in a show I produce."

With that last statement, Sherrie snatched her pocketbook from the ear of the chair she was sitting in and gestured to Charlie they should head back to the office. As they waited for the valet to bring her car, Sherrie took out a pack of cigarettes from her purse, pulled one to her lips and lit it. She took a few puffs and lazily blew smoke out of her lips as she gazed in Charlie's direction. The valet had finally arrived with the car five minutes later, and they drove back to the office with the convertible top down. Charlie returned to the office motivated and spent the rest of the work day reading, analyzing, and familiarizing himself with the Knapp v. Edison case.

He didn't have the advantage of experience and continuity, so he needed to find a way to contribute early and often to stand out above his peers. He figured working after hours, especially on his first day, would curry favor with Sherrie, the hard to please associates, and perhaps even the giant, Mr. Patterson. When 8:00 P.M. rolled around, however, he had had enough. He surmised that three hours of overtime on his first day was a great way to make an early impression.

Seconds after turning off his computer, Charlie stapled a few loose papers together, placed them in an open tray, and stuffed the remaining items in a manila folder in his desk drawer.

Afterwards he stood up, turned off the desk lamp, slipped on his suit jacket, grabbed his leather briefcase, and made his way out the door. The firm's main floor was still humming with activity late into the night, and a few of the firm's committee members were huddled together in deep discussion in the Roosevelt Conference Room. No one looked Charlie's way as he shuffled past them.

Exhausted from a taxing first day, Charlie left the building feeling weary, yet energized. If he had to assess his first day of work, he thought it went swimmingly well, with a few hiccups. Yes, Sherrie was on his mind. Okay, he admitted to himself, Sherrie dominated his thoughts. But he knew better than to push those boundaries and was happy to keep his desires to himself.

At the onset of dawn, Charlie woke up bright eyed and ready for the day ahead. After a stiff yawn and a slow stretch, Charlie headed to the bathroom for a shower. He stepped into the shower, turning to feel the sluice of the water down his back, and allowed the hot water to sooth his aching muscles. Having properly dressed, he sauntered into his kitchen to make himself a cappuccino, and then he headed out the door, cheerfully walking pass several neighboring apartments before reaching his car. Minutes later Charlie's older model Honda Accord merged into heavy traffic before finally reaching the office a quarter to seven.

When Charlie reached the bank of elevators, his phone buzzed in his pocket. He pulled it out of his pocket and quickly examined the number that appeared on the display. It wasn't a phone number he recognized. Curious he picked up the call and was pleasantly surprised by the voice on the other end: it was Sherrie.

"The early bird gets the worm."

"Hi, Sherrie, good to hear your voice. By the way, how did you get my number? I don't remember giving it to you."

"A woman has her ways. Now where are you with the Knapp case?" Sherrie asked.

"I have a lot to catch up on."

"Indeed, you do. Nevertheless, I need your input on the Knapp matter pronto."

"I am only vaguely familiar with the key facts of the case and the court's prior rulings on various motions. I am not sure I know enough to speak in depth."

"Then you better get up to speed by the time I swing by your office in exactly one hour."

Charlie hung up with Sherrie, and with the alacrity of a cheetah, rushed pass reception and directly to his workstation. With little time to spare, he summarily read through the Knapp documents and made an outline of the key concepts he wanted to talk over with Sherrie.

Before he could finish his outline, however, Sherrie was behind Charlie's chair.

Charlie quickly turned around and said, "I think I am ready to debrief."

"You think or you know?" Sherrie questioned. Noticing Charlie squirming in his seat, Sherrie attempted to pacify him, "Don't soil your underwear, I am just giving you a hard time. Michael is anal and wants things done a certain way, or forget about it. I'm of a similar mindset and understand his vision."

Charlie cleared his throat, turned around to face his computer, and began his review of the case. Sherrie remained quiet when he was done. Her body language did not exhibit a hint of emotion either way. With practiced coolness, she rose out of her chair and placed her left hand on Charlie's right shoulder. Charlie couldn't help feel animated by her touch and briefly daydreamed what it would be like to kiss and caress her lips.

Awakening him from his daydream, Sherrie declared, "Looks like you've done your homework. I like everything, except the part that Knapp may survive summary judgment. I believe our summary judgment motion will knock Knapp's case out. You see, Charlie, life is about connections and calling in favors. Michael is not the top partner at the firm because he looks like James Bond, although that would certainly help his cause," Sherrie said, "He's on top because he has cachet and all the judges in his pocket. When he's on a case, it's like having God on your side."

Sherrie removed her hand from Charlie's shoulder, and without a hint of awkwardness, she slid it down his chest and began rubbing it slowly. She kept rubbing his chest until she sensed Charlie was aroused, then abruptly stopped. Charlie was in emotional limbo. He desired Sherrie and had fantasized of this type of interaction with her so many times before, but he was equally confused by her sudden come on. Reading her actions as a signal of her interest in him, he reached for Sherrie's hand to reciprocate, but she nimbly swatted his hand away.

"Slow down, darling. You must get a handle on your emotions."

Embarrassed and confused by her rejection, Charlie stayed silent.

Sherrie switched her attention back to her assessment of Charlie's work as if nothing had happened and said, "You had a good start, but I need you to understand Michael plays for keeps. I need you to research the judge in the Knapp case, the Honorable Pete Seton. I don't care about his educational credentials or civic commitments. I need to know how we can persuade him to see things our way."

"I thought Mr. Patterson had every judge in his pocket."

"Almost every judge. Some are bitten by the impartial justice bug. When that happens, it's up to us to rid them of this despicable and terribly inconvenient fungus. Catch my drift?"

"I believe I do."

"Good, you catch on quick. I don't care to read more paper work, but Michael will want a concrete strategy on Judge Seton first thing in the morning. Have it in my inbox tomorrow before 10:00 A.M. Am I clear?"

"Very," Charlie said.

Pleased with herself, Sherrie smiled and then walked out of Charlie's cubicle.

In the ensuing months, Sherrie and Charlie grew close both professionally and personally. And to his delight, he wasn't imagining Sherrie's interest in him. Harmless flirtations and sexual innuendos led to a burgeoning relationship where romantic getaways and dinners were the norm. One such dinner occasion took place at the Grandeur, a splendid five-star restaurant known for attracting prominent lawyers, celebrities, and high-profile politicians. There they dined on excellent cuisine, sipped leisurely from a $300 bottle of 1976 Pinot Noir, and consummated the date with a romantic moonlight walk along the ocean. The night couldn't have been more flawless, and Charlie couldn't have been any more smitten.

When Charlie pulled up at Sherrie's house, which was located on a quaint block lined with rows of beautiful, picturesque Mediterranean style homes, he hesitated to kiss her. But when their eyes eventually met, he knew it was his moment. Pulling her close, his lips searched for hers. They kissed softly at first, then harder with growing conviction and desire.

"Let's take this inside," Sherrie said softly.

"You sure?"

"Charlie, I've been thinking about this for a while now. Are you going to ask questions, or are you going to come in?"

Charlie and Sherrie made their way in the house, and soon Charlie was eagerly taking off her clothes, but Sherrie held him back.

"Slower," she whispered, "Let our passion dictate the pace. I'm not going anywhere."

Charlie took the cue, slowed down his pace, and began carefully undressing Sherrie. He started with taking off her shoes, then standing her up to remove her top, slowly unzipping her skirt, sliding it to the floor while taking in the view of her shapely legs in the champagne-colored stockings. Caressing her legs, he gently rolled the stockings down and off, pulled Sherrie close, and gently kissed her while he unfastened her lacy bra. He savored the sweetness of her scent, stroking and kissing her thighs, her legs, and her supple breasts. Moments later they were in the thick of it. Day break and the sun's gradual ascent into the clear blue skies signaled the end of a wonderful night passed.

After they helped each other dress, Sherrie said, "Charlie, I'll be out with the girls this evening."

"Oh, okay. What do you girls have planned?" Charlie asked with a hint of disappointment betraying his voice.

"Just regular girl's stuff: shopping, dinner, things of that nature. Why the questions?" Sherrie said slightly annoyed.

"Nothing really, just curious. I'll miss you, that's all."

Sherrie did not reply and hurried toward the door. Before leaving she said, "Oh, Charlie, don't forget to lock the door behind you when you leave later. Like a hotel, your stay here is not unlimited."

"That's cold. I thought we had an understanding I would be here for the weekend."

"That was your understanding, not mine. And how did we get down this road anyway? Soon you'll want to be here every weekend. Look, Charlie, I have a good time when I'm with you, but let's not spoil things with childish frivolity."

With that Sherrie blew him an air kiss and was out the door before Charlie could respond. Charlie was taken aback by Sherrie's terseness but convinced himself to let the matter die.

"Hey, Joe, it's Charlie. What are you up to?"

Joe said, "I have a date with Jessica from Accounting. Why?"

"Nothing really, I was hoping you and I could grab a drink. It's been a long day at the office."

"I wish I could, but tonight's not good. How about some other time?"

A few nights later, Joe and Charlie met at the Fox Hole, a nearby pub midway between Charlie's and Joe's homes. Joe chose the pub for its proximity, as he figured its distance from the office would lessen the chance of encountering someone from the firm there. Joe arrived at the Fox Hole first. Charlie arrived a few minutes after him and spotted Joe already at the bar chatting with a muscular bartender. The pub was crowded with drinking men and women jammed tight around the bar, talking excitably with each other. Charlie casually strolled up to the bar and motioned to the bartender.

"What are you having, my man?" asked the bartender

"A shot of Bourbon, and keep the tab open," Charlie said.

"I'll have a Rusty Nail," Joe chimed in.

The bartender retreated to make their drinks.

"How are things, man?"

"Things couldn't be better," replied Charlie.

"You still ignoring my advice about Sherrie?" Joe said with a half-smile on his face.

"Sherrie is all a man can ask for," Charlie responded defensively. "She's funny, highly intelligent, and don't forget absolutely gorgeous. She's a great woman. You need to lay off her."

Joe's face turned into a frown. "Don't you think you're jumping the gun? You've been together, what, three months?"

"No, it's been nearly six months…and I'm not rushing things. I'm in love with her and see a future with her."

The bartender delivered their drinks.

"Here's to you, bud," wanting to diffuse the tension between them, Joe said, "Cheers." They downed their drinks and felt the burn of the alcohol at the back of their throats. "Charlie, I'm saying this to you because I care. I just think you should be careful with her."

Charlie's face didn't hide his annoyance, "I don't know that I should be taking advice from a self-admitted womanizer."

"That's a cheap shot. I have your best interest in mind."

"How?" Charlie asked. "Every woman you meet, you have some issue with it. Either they're too needy, too many kids, too short, or too boring. No one is ever good enough."

"Look, Charlie, just because I haven't found the right one yet doesn't mean I don't know what I am talking about. I don't believe Sherrie is right for you."

"Well, I believe she's right for me…and that's all that matters. I've been with my share of ladies, and none have come close to making me feel the way Sherrie makes me feel. I think about her all the time: her smell, the feel of her hair, the taste of her lips. I'm crazy about this woman!"

"Man, you got it bad for her." Charlie didn't respond. "And that's what worries me," Joe continued. "You're my friend, and I just don't want to see you get hurt. You're blinded by your desires for her and don't see her for who she really is."

"And you do?" quipped Charlie.

"A lot more than you do right now. You are putting a lot into this relationship. What if Sherrie loses interest and decides to move on from you?"

"Why would she do that?" Charlie said irritated.

"Because I believe she's up to something. Her strong interest in you just doesn't add up. I mean, look at Sherrie. She's used to mingling with high rollers. I-"

"She looks beyond a man's pockets, Joe. Besides you make it sound like I'm some loser or something. Why wouldn't she be interested in someone like me? I'm smart, handsome, and ambitious like her. She knows–"

"Charlie, you're too naïve."

"Listen to yourself. You sound as if you're jealous, bitter that someone like Sherrie is interested in me instead of someone like you," Charlie said.

"No, Charlie, I'm not. You're getting yourself all worked up for this woman and you don't truly know her. She is using you for something. I just don't know what that something is, but she is, my friend."

Angry, Charlie retorted, "You know what? I'm sick of this nonsense." He got up to leave, but Joe grabbed his arm and beckoned for him to sit down. "Where do you get off talking about her like that?"

Attempting to calm Charlie down, Joe lowered his voice, apologized, and switched the topic of their conversation to sports. A few minutes later, the tension dissipated between them, and they had a few more drinks. At a half past 10:00 P.M., Charlie closed out his bar tab, said goodbye to Joe, and headed home for the night.

In subsequent months, Charlie hit several work milestones: he managed a high-profile document review project, was offered a key leadership position on a monumental case, and second chaired his first trial. He was making a name for himself and slowly building his professional brand at the firm. Charlie had become revered for his technical prowess and exacting research skills. Even attorneys outside his department came to him to solve their most complex problems.

Even so Charlie yearned for a more intimate connection with Sherrie, and for whatever reason, he couldn't get past the steady dating stage. The fact was there had been more overtures from her, and the entrusting of the firm's secrets, and even more surprisingly, the sharing of dirt on Mr. Patterson. Each time he appeared to be reeling her in, Sherrie would slip from his grasp and his bewilderment would ensue all over again. Despite this Charlie couldn't get Sherrie out of his mind. He was fascinated by her. In his mind, the signs of a blossoming intimate relationship was all there, if only he knew how to put it all together.

Charlie found himself spending more and more time over at Sherrie's, often to cap out a great work week. During one early morning, when Charlie was at Sherrie's place, her phone rang. Sherrie stirred slowly out of her slumber.

On the third ring, Sherrie picked up her phone and said, "Hello. Oh, hi. May I call you back? This is an awfully inconvenient time. Listen, honey, I have to go."

Charlie, now awake himself, wasn't sure what to make of the surreptitious conversation. He wondered who was on the other end of the conversation.

With his curiosity piqued, he asked, "What was that about?"

"Nothing to worry about, darling," Sherrie said seductively, brushing his question aside, "I have a few things to handle today. Mind if we take a raincheck on seconds? I promise to make it up to you."

Charlie was vexed but let the matter pass, convincing himself he was overreacting. A few months after that incident, there had been another such occurrence, a 3:00 A.M. call. This time he angrily picked up Sherrie's phone, ready to confront the person on the other line, but the caller abruptly hung up, robbing him of the satisfaction of challenging the offender. As a result, his suspicions of Sherrie grew. When Sherrie suggested a Greece vacation to divert Charlie's attention, he eagerly took the bait. Before he knew it, Charlie was packing for their weekend getaway, excited to spend time with Sherrie.

All concerns he had were allayed after the retreat to the Mediterranean paradise. There they basked under the warm sun, ate to their hearts' content, and made love the entire weekend. They spent nights discussing the framework of married life together, and she seemed happy at the idea of becoming his wife, living happily in a charming five-bedroom house atop a hill with a beautiful garden, outdoor swimming pool, with their children frolicking in the backyard with the dogs in tow. He left Greece, convinced the trip solidified their future together.

Unfortunately, it turned out to be short lived bliss. Soon after they returned, the late-night calls continued. Charlie, desperate to win Sherrie's affection, continued to reason away his rising suspicions. He wanted nothing more than for Sherrie to feel for him as he felt for her. To win her heart, he would look for clever ways to deliver on work assignments he and Sherrie were working on together, like the information he dug up on Judge Seton.

Just as the clock hit 9:30 A.M., Michael Patterson poured himself a scotch on the rocks. He lifted the drink to his waiting lips, swirling the ice cubes gently in his glass, took a sip, and smiled. Few occasions called for his favorite scotch—the Dalmore Scotch Single Malt 1973 Constellation Collection Cask from the Highland Region of Scotland yielded $25,000 a bottle—but this moment called for it. Thanks to Sherrie's excellent summary on Judge Seton, he had a clear path forward. The firm had over $25 million riding on the Knapp case, and losing was not an option. To maintain his immortal reputation, victory was not hoped for, it was expected. Thinking of the irrefutable proof he had of Judge Seton's liabilities, he smiled even wider. Convinced he could now vanquish the case via summary judgment, Michael poured himself another scotch on the rocks; this time he savored the drink a little longer and then picked up the phone from its cradle and direct dialed Sherrie.

"Yes, Michael."

"Sherrie, what would I do without you?"

"Shrivel up and die."

"Ha-ha," Michael laughed, "You certainly know how to get to the heart of the matter."

"Listen, I'll have my assistant make dinner plans at Le Rouge tonight at 8:00 P.M. How about I arrange for my driver to be at your place quarter till?"

"Looks like you're in a celebratory mood."

"I have you to thank for that. How did you find such dirt on the Judge?"

"I have my ways. The less you know, the better."

"No truer words have ever been spoken."

Michael and Sherrie kept an apartment on the West side of Los Angeles for their rendezvous. That evening Sherrie was feeling particularly frisky and decided to wear a little black lingerie that left little to the imagination. Michael, at rest in their love palace, was puffing on a vintage 1960s Cohiba cigar when the door opened. Before he took the second puff of his cigar, Sherrie let herself in with her key, and not a moment too soon for Michael's ravenous desire was beginning to unravel.

On the night stand was a small box wrapped in shiny sapphire paper. It contained a silver necklace Michael had bought from Tiffany's. He knew one of Sherrie's well-known weaknesses was luxurious charms. Sherrie walked past Michael over to the antique record player in the living room, put a Frank Sinatra record on, then walked to the bar to pour herself a glass of Cabernet Sauvignon. With her wine in hand, she walked over to Michael, kissed him passionately on the lips, and then walked in the direction of the bedroom. Michael followed, eagerly anticipating what was to take place next. When Michael arrived in the bedroom, Sherrie had undressed entirely and was stretched out on the bed, humming and singing along with the divine Frank.

Sherrie loved being with powerful men like Michael. His power was all the aphrodisiac she needed—and the substantial monthly allowance she received from Michael didn't hurt either. With Michael's many gifts of appreciation, Sherrie could easily afford her home in Tarzana Hills and this apartment, the hideaway she met Michael at once a week, sometimes twice. She also relished the seemingly endless gifts he bestowed upon her: Cartier watches, La Perla lingerie, designer shoes like Christian Louboutin, Tiffany's jewelry, courtside tickets at NBA games, and VIP passes to concerts, to name a few. Michael wasn't much of a lover—she was always relieved when she heard him whimper during their sexual escapades. It meant that soon the old man would roll off her. She liked that he was not one to linger, wanting to whisper sweet nothings in her ears. He just rolled right off, slightly out of breath, and was gone less than an hour later.

"Rebecca will be vacationing in Paris this week, spending all my damn money at an art show again. That wife of mine is more efficient at dispensing cash than an ATM machine," he chuckled to himself. "You're different though. You cost a fortune, too, but it's money well spent—I see the returns on my investment."

Don't get sentimental on me, old man," Sherrie teased.

Michael had a number of problems that had contributed to his relationship with Sherrie, the principal one being that he had not been capable of having a sexual relationship with his wife, Rebecca, of twenty-five years. He had lost interest and had decided his time and money was better spent chasing younger and more exciting skirts like Sherrie.

As he slid his legs into a pair of black trousers and buttoned his suspenders, he asked, "What are we going to do with Charlie? This budding romance has been going on a little too long, don't you think?"

"Darling, I am just having a little fun, that's all. Charlie has been incredibly resourceful, remember Knapp?"

"How could I forget," Michael said, smiling widely.

"That's why I had human resources personally recruit him; I knew he would come through. His research skills are beyond anyone's I've encountered; he's genius personified. But I understand the risk and know the time to cut bait is now. Pity, I was really beginning to enjoy the charade," Sherrie said.

Michael stopped tying his tie and turned around to look at Sherrie. She was still lying on the bed, uncovered and naked, and Frank Sinatra was singing "I Did it My Way" in the background. Sherrie was beautiful and a killer in the sack. It never bothered him that she came with a hefty price tag. The Sinatra record ended. Sherrie swallowed the last of her wine. Before she knew it, Michael was dressed, in the garage, backing out his $200,000 midnight blue Mercedes, speeding away to his next destination. And Sherrie thought to herself, *Just the way I like it.*

After Michael's departure, Sherrie walked to her bathroom, turned on the shower, and was ready to enter when she heard footsteps up the stairs. She draped herself with the silk robe that was hanging on the hook near the shower. She left the bathroom and walked to the door, peered through the peep hole, and saw that the person on the other side of the door was Charlie.

How does he know to find me here? Sherrie thought, I must have told him.

Sherrie opened the door and let Charlie in. Without a word, Charlie walked past her towards the living room. When Sherrie reached the living room's doorway, Charlie was standing by the fireplace, peering into the flames. Charlie looked at Sherrie in the doorway and shook his head at her disapprovingly. Sherrie pretended not to notice the anguished look on his face and moved across the room to meet him by the fireplace.

Sherrie kissed him on his right cheek, caressing his shoulders while removing his suit jacket. To her surprise, Charlie did not contest, and she proceeded to remove his tie, took his hands in hers and led Charlie to the kitchen. The room remained quiet before Sherrie broke the impasse.

"What are you thinking about?" Sherrie asked.

"About a woman I used to know named Kelly."

"What of her are you thinking about, darling?" she asked as she poured him a glass of vodka.

Charlie took the glass from Sherrie, closed his eyes, and drained his vodka. He walked away from her and began his soliloquy, "The summer we spent together was majestic. We were just out of high school, trying to figure life out together. When you spend a few close months with someone, you can really get to know them. She was my first love, and I broke her heart. It's funny, I didn't understand it at the time."

"Where is this going?" Sherrie interrupted.

Ignoring Sherrie, Charlie continued, "Kelly was sweet, honest, loyal, and committed. A devoted—"

"Don't say another word. You sound very tired, darling. Let me get you another drink."

"Make it a double; we're in for a long night," Charlie said, briefly breaking his monologue. After a brief pause, Charlie continued, "Kelly never lied to me, never betrayed my trust, never abused me, or took me for granted."

Sherrie returned to the living room to where Charlie was now standing and said, "And I haven't either."

"The hell you haven't!" Charlie yelled.

He headed to the kitchen to pour himself another glass of vodka.

"Don't you walk away from me, Charlie. You tell me what's going on."

"What's going on? The arrogance of you. Should I spell it out?"

"Why don't you be a man for once and just speak up?"

Charlie stared angrily at Sherrie, "I expected so much more from you. I thought we had something special."

"That's the problem with you, darling, you think too much."

"I've been keeping track of your secret rendezvous with Michael."

"Now you're a private eye? Any other little secrets I need to know about?" Sherrie said sarcastically.

"Don't turn this one me," Charlie said indignantly. "I have it on good account you and Michael have been carrying on an illicit affair for quite some time."

Sensing her ruse was up, Sherrie admitted, "Illicit is such a strong word. Don't you mean we've been carrying on a consensual relationship?"

"How could you do this to me, Sherrie?"

"I'll admit it, Charlie. I like you. We had some good times together. But Michael is a unique man, not to mention powerful and highly influential. I'm attracted to men like him, men who can make the world bow down to them, and offer me unparalleled access to the most important and influential people in the world." Sherrie paused for a moment and then strolled a few steps away from him, "Don't you see, Charlie. Men like Michael don't associate with men like you. You two don't travel in the same universe and never will. The mere fact you two shared the same building, let alone the same floor, means the Gods have looked down kindly on you."

"You are a cruel, heartless person! You carried on with Michael without a care for my feelings. And for what?"

Sherrie stared at him and said with cocky coolness, "For a penthouse apartment, a house in the hills, a $100,000 BMW convertible, $25,000 in monthly allowance and access."

"The devil bought your soul."

"Michael is hardly the devil," Sherrie chuckled. "He's my kind of man."

"An old, brooding, miserable man. That's what you need in your life?"

"Look, Charlie, the end is here. We had a good run, and now we must go our separate ways. It's nothing personal."

"You can't be serious," Charlie said, "I thought we were building something together.

"It was a mirage, Charlie. I needed your skills and connections. A woman like me can't be kept by someone like you. Look, darling, you're a good guy. You have a great heart, a true gentleman. But I'm a head lioness."

"And Michael is what...the king of the jungle?"

"Precisely. I've always said you catch on quick."

"Don't patronize me."

"Patronizing you is far from what I'm doing. I appreciated your service and commitment to the cause. We couldn't have taken care of the Knapp matter without your shrewd maneuvering. The info you found on the judge was priceless."

"I don't care for your praises. I've had enough of the games! I need to know now where our relationship stands, Sherrie."

"Darling, have another drink, it will settle you."

With his anger and frustration boiling over, Charlie slapped the glass of vodka out of Sherrie's hands.

"Enough!"

"Okay. I suppose I owe you an explanation, to give you the state of things, don't I, Charlie?"

"That's the least you can do."

"Michael serves my needs and a purpose in my life right now. He is nearly seventy-years-old and has been married for decades to the same stiff. He's lonely and bored. His wife is a philanthropist, spends his millions on various stupid charities just to fill her time up and give purpose to her dreary life. He was dead before I came into his life. Because of me, he's been revived and his life now has meaning."

"So, you're his caretaker?"

"I'm his reason for living."

"Aren't you modest," Charlie said sarcastically.

"Enough with your sarcasm and self-righteousness. You're acting like a naive brat." Sherrie opened a nearby draw where she kept a pack of cigarettes. She retrieved the pack, pulled one to her lips, and lit the cigarette. She also tilted out a glass of vodka for herself before continuing, "I am no good for you, darling. Yes, we had good times, but the moment has passed. You must understand that." In a moment of desperation, Charlie reached for Sherrie's left arm, but she moved away. "This is goodbye, Charlie."

"Please don't leave me, Sherrie."

"Darling, the decision has already been made. It's time you go home now. I have things to do and places to go."

The distraught expression in Charlie's eyes shocked Sherrie and made her avert her eyes.

"Au revoir, Charlie."

And with that last remark, Sherrie closed the door on Charlie and walked out of his life forever.

Charlie returned to the office the next day and attempted to finish his work assignments, but his thoughts were troubled. The incident with Sherrie kept playing on a loop in his mind. He kept asking himself why had he ignored the signs that appeared throughout his involvement with her. He couldn't understand why he allowed himself to be so gullible and taken for a ride like this. Emotionally tortured, bereavement led Charlie to leave work early for his home, and this started a chain of devastating events, which lead to his complete unraveling.

In short order, his life became a downward spiral to hell. Things that had seemed important, or that carried meaning in his life, no longer did. Distraught and grieved beyond console, Charlie stopped eating, caring for his appearance, and wasn't sleeping. His work product began to suffer at the firm. He was continuously tardy or absent, and eventually he was fired.

Charlie drank heavily to numb his grief, consuming dangerous amounts of alcohol on a daily basis. He spent most days secluded, barely sleeping three hours a night, and watching too much television. Eating became a terrible chore. When he did manage to eat, he had trouble holding much of it down. He felt as if he couldn't go on anymore, and one day Charlie gave in to these desires.

DEATH'S SEDUCTIVE VOICE MEOWED THROUGH THE FRONT DOOR, and he took notice. As a heavy rainstorm saturated the city streets, Charlie Black stood quietly at the entrance of his drab living room, absentmindedly staring at a blank wall while contemplating suicide. He'd been hashing out the fine details of his death for a while, and this solemn day seemed ripe for the offering. With options limited, friends and family proving useless—they ran away at any signs of trouble—and with weekly head shrink visits pushing him closer to the edge, Charlie felt shattered.

While he fiddled with his thoughts, the ferocious rainstorm drenched the metropolis, dispersing large swaths of raging water across the weather-beaten city. The storm had reached near full strength, and with each passing moment, it grew angrier and more encompassing. Despite the brewing pandemonium outside, it was eerily quiet inside his apartment. Neither the sound of an adult neighbor's random conversation nor the voices of children frolicking in the background could be heard, just dead silence. Amid the silence, Charlie took stock of the chaos before him, and what he witnessed left an indelible impression. Over a period of weeks, he'd created a mess where littered breadcrumbs, dirty floors, unwashed dishes, and loads of dirty laundry were the norm.

With his veneer of calm completely fractured, Charlie's face was a dual mask of pain and distress. Due to inattentiveness, his normally well-manicured face now sported a growing stubble, which spread across his face like contagion. To add to the unsightliness, his hair was grossly unkempt. Grease residue permeated his hair, and his lack of bathing created films of unsightly dandruff on his scalp. Charlie's clothing was in tatters. His favorite blue jeans had a two-inch hole in the crotch. His white sneakers were dirty and badly faded, the once distinguished Nike logo a thing of the past.

As day drifted into night and the once mighty rainstorm abated to a light mist, Charlie picked up a black and white portrait of his parents from his coffee table. The picture was a little less for wear, but he could clearly make out the incandescent smiles of his parents. Young and in the prime of their lives, his parents' faces were idyllic. He brought the photo closer and slowly wiped away the dust bunnies that had accumulated and found himself being transported back to random childhood memories.

His mother had lived a life full of hope and promise. She was the image of beauty and elegance. Charlie's father also dazzled in the photo. At 6'4", his father was a giant among his peers. A former weightlifter and wrestler, his father had reveled in his short-lived fame as a top high school athlete.

When his father, Paul, reminisced about his youth, which he did ad nauseum, he would boast, "Those girls were stuck on me like white on rice."

His parents were madly in love once. When they met, Elena, Charlie's diminutive mother, was a straight A high school junior with college aspirations. Elena did not suffer fools well, and generally had no patience for immature people, especially one of Paul's ilk. This made it more surprising that the well-known bookworm and self-admitted prude would fall so easily in love with a blowhard blunderer like Paul. His mom would often warmly recount the story of how she and his father met.

He could hear her fondly saying to him and his siblings, "Your father was dancing with another girl when I walked by in my little yellow sundress and dazzling smile. When we locked eyes, the rest was history. I knew then that your father and I were bound by destiny. It was like no one else mattered. And your father hasn't once left my side since that chance encounter. I suppose when I think about it now, we were kindred spirits."

Over both families' vigorous objection, Paul and Elena hitched in hum drum fashion at city hall in front of one family witness, a distant cousin of Paul's who was cajoled into the role for an exchange of favors. Before the ink dried on their marriage certificate, Paul and Elena began unloading babies. Elena gave birth to their first son, Bryan, a bright but ill-behaved child. After a surprisingly easy labor, Sandy, the precious apple of his father's eye, was introduced to the world. Sandy did not utter a peep after leaving her mother's womb and instead stared right at Paul, smiled, and spoke the words "Dada"—at least that's the folly Charlie's dad wanted people to believe.

Charlie was born a year after Sandy. As Charlie grew into adulthood, he remained the center of his mother's universe. He was unabashedly a momma's boy, and he loved it. The bond between he and his mom was quite evident, and Elena didn't give a damn which of her two other children felt slighted by the extra attention and love she showered on her little Charlie. Charlie sighed and thought to himself, *Those were the good old days, a time when family meant everything and they had each other's backs.*

The memories brought Charlie to tears, and he again thought to himself, *Where did it all go wrong?*

As more recollections came to mind, Charlie remembered Sunday dinners as a thing of magnificent glee. His mom's feasts were exquisite—a fanciful feast of rice and beans, stewed chicken, roasted vegetables, and for dessert, a family favorite, freshly baked apple pie with two servings of whip cream. The gatherings were held in the compact family dining room where the Black clan would promptly gather at 5:00 P.M. Tardiness was a cardinal sin in Elena's eyes, and she simply wouldn't tolerate it. You were either promptly seated at the table by dinner time or faced her volcanic wrath, the rare occasion when she would lose her cool. His dad sat at the head of a small wood table; his mom was perched to his left, and the kids, Bryan, Sandy, and Charlie, filled in the remaining seats based on seniority. That was the order of things, and the seating arrangements never changed, no matter the circumstances.

Despite the rigid seating accommodations, family conversations were surprisingly fluid, lively, and humorous. Paul, who had a wonderful wit and an extraordinary skill for absurdity, often held court. He was a fabulous raconteur and dazzled everyone with countless hilarious stories of his exploits during his wild youth. One such story recalled a time Paul took his father's prized red Porsche out for a joy ride without permission and plowed the fabled car into a neighbor's garage, leaving a trail of bedlam along the way. Paul's taskmaster dad, Ben Black, a colossal man with fiery temper, was furious and inconsolable. Paul's betrayal was too much for Charlie's grandfather to stomach, and as a means of reprimand, Ben banished Paul to months of hard labor. Paul was compelled to work day and night during one scorching summer to pay for the repair work to the Porsche and the neighbor's garage. Unfortunately, the moral of crime and punishment was lost on Charlie's dad, and he continued his rebellious ways well into his adulthood.

Unlike Paul, Elena was humble by nature, thoughtful, giving, a nurturer to a fault, and an avoider of the spotlight. The less the light shined on her, the better. However, Elena would often come to life during meal time conversations, holding court, and displaying a mastery of storytelling that fascinated her children but annoyed her husband. When Elena got into her storytelling mojo, it was like a freight train on a direct path to its destination: purposeful, full of life lesson goodies, and there was no stopping her. For his dad, the attention seeker, Elena sharing the spotlight was too much to bear.

Without fail he'd interrupt her with snide comments like, "Elena, it's not nice to hog up all the time. Other people would like to say something, too."

Charlie and his siblings would also participate in dinner time conversations, as his mom would make it a point to ask each one of them about their day. She'd listen intently, hanging on their every word, offering encouragement where needed, and howled in laughter, even when their jokes were far from funny.

But not all of Charlie's recollections about his childhood that fateful night was joyful. The dreaded family chores made sure of that. The misery took place every Saturday, which was errands and cleaning day at the Black home. On Saturdays his mom awoke at 5:00 A.M. sharp without fail. After her usual stretch, Elena alighted from her bed and kneeled at the edge with her hands clasped in front of her in a prayer offering to God. From there she'd slip on her pink furry slippers and matching bathrobe and headed to the kitchen to prepare a pot of coffee. She poured her black, sugarless coffee into a large mug, and then placed herself in her favorite chair, the one with the distinguished pink flower design.

Elena would meticulously categorize her grocery list into various food groups: meat, dairy, vegetables, fruits, bread, and desserts. After the grocery list was to her liking, she'd peruse through various newspapers for coupons, clipping out a dozen or so until satisfied she had the right combination to realize the enormous savings she sought. Task done she'd stuff the coupons into her black utility handbag and left it on the table before retreating to the bathroom to get ready for the day ahead. She'd enter the shower humming love ballads and seventies classics. After she showered, Elena dressed in a blur of efficiency.

His mom would often arrive at Savings Plus Supermarket at 6:00 A.M., dressed in her favorite dark blue jeans and black cotton sweater, an outfit that had fit her since her freshman year in high school. Without wasted effort, she'd commandeer the nearest shopping cart and put her carefully laid grocery plan to work, displaying an uncanny level of proficiency locating and selecting the items on her list at the lowest possible price. Within the hour, Elena's shopping cart was full, and she was ready to check out.

By 6:45 A.M., like clockwork, she would come barreling down the driveway, horns blaring, calling for everyone to help. To the family's chagrin, her weekly ritual meant the cessation of sleep for all members of the Black household, except for his dad. The grouch stubbornly refused to leave the comforts of his bed, and after countless arguments on the matter, Elena and Paul finally brokered a truce, which meant Elena begrudgingly agreeing to leave him be so long as Paul promised to handle other specified house chores. Of course, Paul almost never kept his word as he was an unrepentant liar, and their short-lived peace customarily disintegrated into week long spats.

At one point, Elena became so violently irate that she said, "Paul, I should know better than to trust anything you say. Your promises aren't worth a damn, and I don't know why I even bother with you. You're like a child in a grown man's body. Every time I put stock in you, I'm disappointed with the results."

Elena was so beside herself with anger that she dug her nails into Paul's arm, contorting his skin in such a manner that it drew blood.

Agitated his dad spat back, "I'm tired of your nagging, and you need to keep your hands off me or else."

"Or else what, Paul Black? You going to hit me? You don't have the guts, you coward. You were never man enough to do anything."

That little jab, that direct challenge to his manhood, had his dad in a fit of rage.

"Dammit, Elena! There you go again…when are you going to stop questioning my manhood and show me some respect as the head of this house? I've done so much for this family."

"Cut the pretense, Paul. Head of household is earned in my book. You haven't been anything close to the father and husband this family needs."

While Paul and Elena were engaged in their war of words, Charlie remembered how immensely sad he felt hearing his parents argue, sobbing softly in his bedroom, wishing they would stop. Tucking away the memories of his parents' battles into the recess of his mind, Charlie's thoughts turned to his siblings. Just the idea of them left him feeling uneasy. Charlie's relationship with his brother was semi-cordial at best, and at worst, like two warring factions preparing for a protracted battle.

Not that he did not find any redeemable qualities in his brother Bryan, it was just that the two did not see eye to eye on much of anything. Bryan, three years his senior, bullied and teased him unmercifully until Charlie became old enough to defend himself. Their fist fights were bloody. Bryan and Charlie often came out of their violent encounters with black eyes, bruises, and bloody noses. However, despite their tumultuous and violent relationship growing up, Bryan was fiercely protective of Charlie. He once beat up a boy who was bullying him so severely, Charlie found himself having to play peacemaker, pulling his brother off the boy, for he feared Bryan would kill him. In their teen years, Bryan and Charlie could engage in a fight and make up the next day. Now, as adults, their relationship was so strained, they hadn't spoken in years.

His relationship with his sister was a bit more complicated. He and Sandy were extremely close at one point. Charlie and his sister were a year apart in age but were in the same grade. Their parents held Sandy back a year, so they could enroll the siblings in school together. Because of this, both siblings benefited tremendously from each other's presence. Where he was barely passable in subjects, like math and science, Sandy was a whiz at them. And when she struggled with English and history, Charlie helped her through them. They took turns doing each other's homework, writing each other's essays and providing answers to exams, and finagled their way through middle school and most of high school. They almost always managed to sit next to each other in every class, so they could pull off their heist. When their teachers became suspicious of their arrangement, Charlie and Sandy took to using secret codes to communicate.

The crack in their relationship began as Sandy blossomed from a geeky adolescent girl with acne and boyish looks to a stunning teenage beauty. When that happened, she was no longer interested in having her little brother hang around her. They continued to grow further apart as they grew older. Despite repeated attempts on Charlie's part to mend things between them, the frost over their relationship never thawed and remains until this day.

Charlie was snapped back to his dreary living room with Sherrie's harrowing image in his mind, hastening his anxiety and dread. From the start, he knew Sherrie was unique. She was the only non-lawyer employee at the firm he knew who commanded as much respect and admiration as the senior male partners. He found her ability to stand on her own endearing, but he had carelessly overlooked less redeemable qualities, such as the measured, calculated ways she controlled everything and everyone around her. Despite warnings from Joe Pascal, urging him to steer far away from her, and other cautionary signs, Charlie had wanted nothing more than the successful progression of his romantic relationship with Sherrie.

How could she have deceived him so easily? Even with his pressing concerns, he had rationalized away all of Sherrie's shortcomings. He yearned to create his own family unit with her so badly that he wouldn't allow himself to see it coming: the set-up, the pumping him for information on Judge Senton, a distant relative, the way she spent many evenings peppering him with questions on Judge Seton's personal life, expertly persuading Charlie to get a hold of a secret record, hidden from public sight, for her.

Here Charlie was thinking Sherrie really loved him. He believed in their relationship and trusted that their talks of getting married and starting a family were genuine. Sherrie had convinced him that her truest desire was a life of blissful domestication, that this "head bitch" act was just something she concocted to compete in the "world of wolves where insecure men too often got all the credit on the backs of the meek women who did all the work. "He ignored all of his instincts and fell so easily for it. A knife through the heart would have been better than what Sherrie did to him; it would have hurt less.

Charlie took stock of his current situation. Frightened he searched for a flicker of sunshine behind the ominous skies. His life's failures, however, left him feeling bitter and dejected, and his body trembled as if besieged by winter's wrath. He harked back to a time when he had thrived under the careful guidance and love of his mom. She was the guiding light in his world when she was alive. Elena constantly worked to show him and his siblings the importance of hard work and the value of treating family and strangers alike with kindness. Though he had been spoiled by his mom, Elena's discipline also kept him in line.

Delving into his mother's positive influence on him, Charlie recalls his college sophomore year. His school grades were abysmally poor, and he was facing expulsion if his grades didn't improve exponentially. Out of rope, it was his mom who saved him. Elena sat him down one chilly Friday morning and told Charlie, in her most strident voice, that under no circumstances would she accept his quitting or getting expelled from college. She had spent the semester helping Charlie tap into the greatest gifts she felt he possessed: his natural intelligence and ability to absorb large volume of information.

HIS MOM'S TOUGH LOVE AND BELIEF IN HIM WAS THE MOTIVATION he needed. He desperately wanted to make his mom proud and became a model student midway through the semester. He managed to turn his failing semester of Ds and Fs to As and Bs. He kept this momentum throughout his collegiate career and ultimately graduated with honors and on schedule all because of his mom.

He could still hear Elana's soothing voice saying, "Charlie, always face life with grace and never give up. For behind every dark cloud, there's a silver lining."

For a time, Charlie had believed this and had spent his life living by his mother's motto. But he wasn't so sure anymore. He lived his life full of grace, but what did that get him? A stab in the back by a duplicitous witch, and now a life in shambles. Where was the silver lining in that? Now that he was moments away from taking his own life, an act his mother, Elena, would surely agree is dishonorable and disgraceful, he breathed a sigh a relief for he knew his act would bear no witness. No Elena, not a soul to cast a judgmental eye or word.

At 7:25 P.M., Charlie sat up from the couch, his stomach tied in knots as he pushed toward the kitchen. There he turned on the overhead lights, took a deep breath, and prayed silently to the heavens. Done with his prayer, he traced the cross sign over his heart. Now on the move, he felt the weight of each agonizing step, and his pulse accelerated. As seeds of doubt crept in, his body began to sweat profusely. He tried valiantly to compose himself and his unsettled nerves but was unsuccessful. Although renewed fear of his imminent death plagued his mind, he remained certain suicide was the only way out of this miserable, callous world.

A few minutes later, the moment had arrived. No longer at a crossroad, Charlie ingested a handful of Percocet and chased down the drug with two cans of beer and three shots of vodka. For a moment, time stood still. But soon the cocktail germinating within him began its ravaging effect. Weakened, Charlie beelined for the couch, convinced his final fate awaited him there. But before he managed his next step, all hell broke loose as the toxins proved devil's play.

As his heart walloped furiously inside his chest, terror, and then panic set in. At long last, and like a leaf blowing freely through the air, Charlie's body and spirit fully succumbed. Steps away from his couch, Charlie fell like a log through the small coffee table, shattering the table's inch thick glass into countless pieces. His unconscious body, which lay spread-eagle, was punctured by numerous shards of glass. Blood oozed from both arms, his neck, and legs. The injuries to his body seemed immeasurable, and his heart commenced to shut down, along with other vital organs.

Charlie was in a desperate state, barely clinging to life with his mind travelling in and out of the conscious world.

Unbeknownst to Charlie, his neighbor, Raymond, heard the loud racket when he fell through his coffee table and rushed upstairs. Raymond knocked on Charlie's door and called out his name numerous times. After no answer from Charlie, Raymond couldn't shake the feeling something was seriously wrong. He knocked a few more times before finally deciding to kick through Charlie's front door. To his dismay, he came in to Charlie's 180-pound body slumped on the living room floor, his face pale, breathing shallow, chest wet with vomit, and blood oozing from various parts of his body. Raymond was screaming into Charlie's ears, dousing him with ice cubes and water and pinching him as his respiratory system began to collapse.

Raymond knew he had precious moments to respond. Rather than wait for an ambulance, Raymond wrapped Charlie's wounds with clean towels, dragged Charlie's body to his car, and raced toward the nearest hospital. When they finally arrived at St. Mary's emergency room, a sea of nurses and medical professionals rushed to Charlie's aid.

The first day of his hospital stay, Charlie vacillated in and out of consciousness. During his unconscious state, ferocious nightmares pervaded Charlie's mind. One for certain was the most far-reaching; it was stronger in its ferocity, misery, and relentlessness. In his reverie, Charlie was alone on an empty road, lost in his thoughts when he wandered into a graveyard. He called out to a figure in the distance who he believed resembled his mother, Elena. When she didn't answer his call, Charlie started to run towards her. But the faster he ran; the more distance grew between them.

Then suddenly he heard a voice calling out to him. He looked back and saw a ghostly skinny woman, and with her, she brought twin sisters: fear and destruction. Their faces were covered with blood, their nails were very long, and they were wearing long, white, shapeless night gowns. Charlie was so frightened by their images that he found himself paralyzed. He saw them rushing towards him, but he still could not move. They stretched their long arms to grab him, laughing at the same time. The horrible screeching sound of their laughter was so loud, it pierced his eardrums. He found his body turning cold and his ears in pain from the cacophony. Just before they could grab him, Charlie made a desperate effort to run, but his feet were stuck in thick mud and he could not move. As they came closer, Charlie screamed loudly in fear. As he was screaming, his eyes cracked open.

Charlie awoke from his vegetative state, covered in a cold sweat, shaking, and his heart pounding. Still trying to shake off his haze, he noticed someone was in the room with him. A matronly woman came to Charlie's assistance. She had gentle eyes and a calming presence.

She walked deliberately over to him, held his hands firmly, and said in a reassuring voice, "Everything will be okay. We are going to take care of you."

Charlie continued suspiciously looking around the room for a clue of where he was before finally realizing he was in the hospital. He was hooked up to an IV drip, a heart monitor, and had an oxygen mask on his face. His back whimpered in complaint from soreness created from lying flat and motionless for days. Charlie remained awake for a few more minutes and then gradually fell back to sleep. He slept through the night and was awaken the next day by a discomfort on his right side. The right side of his body began to itch violently as if attacked by an army of mosquitoes. When he tore open his hospital garment to temper the itch, much like a scampering rabbit, it leapt to another part of Charlie's body. Realizing the futility of his efforts, Charlie eased his limp body further into his bed and yielded to the prickliness.

Thankfully his hospital room was kept cool. The ancient air conditioner blew a steady and even flow of cool air throughout the room. Aside for the noise spewing from the old air conditioner, the beeps from the machines attached to him, and the persistent ticking of the wall clock that hung on the wall a few feet across his bed, activity on the hospital floor was surprisingly muted. As the days passed, however, the clock's ticking grew louder and louder, exacerbating his self-loathing and feelings of isolation. Restless from idleness, Charlie turned on the night lamp, slowly sat up, and reached for the book he saw on his hospital bed table. The book was ironically a novel titled, "Moving on from Heartache." Intrigued, Charlie read the dust jacket cover and discovered the novel was about a man who tragically lost everything before managing to get his life back together against all odds. Despite his interest in the subject, the book touched on a topic too close to home. He had not been able to get his life back in order and was still struggling with his own psychological demons. The idea that others had been able to do what he could not angered him. In disgust Charlie hurled the novel across the room.

Charlie then turned on the television and impatiently channel surfed through what seemed like hundreds of shows before settling on one with a motivational bent to it. The speaker, a dashing older gentleman with salt and pepper hair, captivated him. His message resonated; it was clear and practical.

And for a moment during the show, Charlie thought the man was speaking to him directly when he said, "Take hold of your life, young man. Obstacles and failures are only one of the many stops in life's journey. Don't stay at those train stations for too long; otherwise, you will miss your final destination."

Moments later the speaker concluded the program with a few parting words of wisdom before departing backstage. Charlie turned the television off and slipped underneath his warm blankets. He was gradually settling in, and as he neared sleep, the sound of heavy snoring jolted him awake. The offender, a nearby patient, was a large White man with a bushy beard and huge belly. He had been in the hospital for treatment of an undisclosed nature. The poor chap almost never came off his bed. He slept often and snored louder than a hibernating bear. Charlie, frustrated, folded a pillow around his head and ears, believing the pillow a buffer to the man's egregious snoring. That effort, unfortunately, proved futile, and Charlie begrudgingly accepted his fate: he was in for a long and certainly unpleasant evening.

Day five of his hospital stay, Charlie was starting to feel a little normal again. He was finally free of the IV needle that was in his arm and was no longer attached to a litany of monitoring devices. Eager to handle basic routines without the aid of a medical professional, Charlie lifted damp blankets off his body and slowly descended from his hospital bed. He turned on the overhead lights. The lights came on dimly at first, flickering twice before eventually catching on. He was tired, sore, and worn down. His hospital pajamas were drenched in perspiration, and droplets of sweat fashioned small puddles across his body. As Charlie moved around to stretch his strained muscles, his knees and ankles whimpered in protest. Laboring to the bathroom, Charlie gently pushed open the door, closed it slowly behind him, and then turned the light switch on.

Viewing his face in the mirror, he was aghast. He noticed a quarter-sized knot had formed on his right temple and that a prior stubble had morphed into a small forest. Feeling an urge to take care of business, he used the lavatory's grab bars to fortify himself and to take pressure off his swollen limbs before slowly lifting the toilet seat. Steadying his aim, he released the contents of his bladder into the toilet bowl. Relieved, Charlie laid the toilet seat down, strolled gingerly toward the door, and turned the lights off. He trekked back to his disheveled bed where the bedsheets rested untidily on the floor.

In a flash, a troubling headache overcame him like darkness after a retiring sunset. Fatigued and with his head aching, he grabbed the two aspirins the nurse left on the nearby table just within arm's reach, and chased the contents down with warm water. A half-hour later, the pesky headache relented, and he was sound asleep. When he finally came to, he sat still for a few seconds, staring at the bland, blue walls wondering, *Why was I here? What did this mean for the rest of my life? How had things become so bleak? Did all my life's accomplishments amount to nothing? What should I do now?* Endless questions circled, but he felt lost in the whirlwind of his mind and at his wit's end as to how to deal with the gravity of his situation.

Aside from visits from his neighbor Raymond, who would sit and talk with him for hours on end, Charlie still felt as though he had no one to buffer the agony he felt. Reprieve finally came in the form of Susan Henderson, the nurse charged with his well-being and recovery.

Ironically the day Susan entered his room was cheerfully clear and sunny, yet Charlie was in one of the darkest points in his life. Susan walked quietly to his bedside that day, silently observing Charlie's chest move up and down.

After a while, she looked Charlie in the eyes and said, "Don't give up hope. You could have died, but you didn't. You're alive, and that is a blessing. Few people make it after a situation like that; you're one of the fortunate ones."

A soft sob emitted from Charlie's chapped lips as he buried his head in his hands. Susan exited the room and returned with a tray full of nourishments—wheat toast, scrambled eggs, orange juice, a packet of butter, and a hot cup of English tea. She carefully placed the food tray in front of Charlie, removing the plastic sheet from the utensils, and used the plastic knife to lightly butter his toast. She took caution not to oversaturate the bread with butter. Susan then placed the eggs between the buttered toast and handed Charlie the final creation.

"Here's your egg sandwich," she said. Charlie barely stirred. Undeterred, Susan gently said, "You must eat, Charlie. Sustenance is very important to your recovery and you need some food in you."

He finally relented and took the sandwich from her waiting hands. Charlie took a small bite at first, then another. Before long the egg sandwich was ancient history. He took a few sips of his orange juice, wiped his mouth with his free hand, and then burped loudly.

Susan beamed. "Burping is a good sign. Have some tea before it cools; it will help with your digestion," she said.

"Got any honey for the tea?" Charlie asked.

"Well of course. How many packets of honey would you like? One? Two?"

"One is fine."

Charlie's mood began to brighten a smidge. He found himself enjoying the food, and more importantly, Susan's company. Susan poured some honey into his tea, using a spoon to mix the contents in the cup.

"Why don't you taste it to make sure it's to your liking," said Susan as she handed Charlie the cup of tea. Charlie received the cup from Susan, sipped the English tea and with a half-smile said, "It's perfect, thank you."

SUSAN SAT ON A RECLINER NEXT TO HIS BED AND WATCHED AS Charlie finished his tea. Charlie nodded in her direction. He was pleased she was staying with him. During his convalescence, several nurses attended to his care, but Susan was his favorite. She seemed to care about more than his physical well-being. Susan took stock of his mental outlook and made it her personal mission to connect with him on a deeper level than what was customary between a nurse and patient.

During his stay at St. Mary's Hospital, Charlie grew close to Susan Henderson. Through numerous conversations, he learned she was in her late sixties and a soap opera junkie. Susan was slightly pudgy, but she shared that recent vigorous workouts had done the trick of reducing her weight a bit. She had amazing red chubby cheeks and frizzy gray hair, which she almost always wore in a bun. She also had stunning hazel eyes that were rare in their radiance and were breathtaking to behold.

On the days she had free time, they talked like two long-time friends who had all the time in the world. Susan told him she had married a young, gregarious medical student in England when she had been studying abroad at the University of Bristol. His name was John Henderson. She recounted to Charlie that she had been a timid nineteen-year-old, soon to be sophomore, and very attractive. John had courted her unabashedly, which had both alarmed and stirred something in her.

That summer in England, he had invited Susan to visit his family in Birmingham. They had a torrid romance and were married weeks later. She returned to the States to finish her education, and John remained in England to complete his medical residency. After she completed her studies, Susan returned to England, to John, and they had four children. The four kids were born rather close together. Susan relayed they were all highly successful in their own rights as adults. Her eldest daughter was a pediatrician at Bellevue Memorial, a small hospital located a few miles outside the downtown district. The youngest child, the second daughter, was a middle school teacher at an all-girls private school in New Jersey. Susan also had two sons, one of whom was a junior attorney with a small law practice in Chicago; the other, a dentist with a growing practice in

Washington. Her husband, unfortunately, had died two years earlier due to complications of pancreatic cancer.

"Charlie, I'll let you in on something I didn't originally share with you. I had five kids. The youngest of them, Mark, committed suicide a year ago. His death shattered everything in me. Although it wasn't easy, I am slowly recovering from the pain of losing him." Hearing Susan's story, Charlie couldn't help but be transported to memories of his own mother, Elena. Charlie snapped back into the room when he heard Susan say, "Oftentimes my own irrationality got in the way of my progress, when sound reasoning and faith would have expedited my healing," she said. "You have to have faith, Charlie," Susan continued. "The heartache you feel may perhaps stay with you for the rest of your life, but you will get through the pain. I am living proof. After losing my son, I thought the dark days would never end, but they did. Each day the sun shined in my life a little bit more."

LISTENING TO SUSAN'S STORY ON HOW SHE EVENTUALLY NAVIGATED her grief stimulated a glimmer of hope in Charlie that he did not think existed anymore. All her parables of life and the lessons of self-worth, dignity, perseverance, and personal accountability gave him the desire to want to rise from the ashes of his life.

Days after his final noteworthy conversation with her, with the sun rays piercing through his hospital room window and the hospital floor buzzing with activity, Susan entered Charlie's room with a discharge notice. Though she was elated for Charlie and genuinely pleased to see him on the road to recovery, she couldn't help feeling morose. She knew it was imprudent to be so attached to a patient, to let personal feelings cloud her judgment, but she couldn't help it. Charlie was delicate and seemed to have a golden soul, like her beloved son, Mark. Something about his spirit and character, notwithstanding his personal calamity, inspired and renewed her sense of purpose.

This past year at the hospital had been particularly difficult for Susan: the emotional scars from her son's death, the grinding daily routine, the administrative red tape, the long hours, internal conflicts, and staff shortages had worn on her. She had been disheartened by it all; notwithstanding her agonizing grief and the guilt she felt over not being able to do more to save her son. Nursing Charlie back to health made her feel as if she was nursing her Mark back to health.

Finding her bearings, Susan looked resignedly at Charlie and said, "Dr. Finkelman is pleased with your progress. He doesn't see any reason why you shouldn't leave today. We ran a battery of tests and everything came back great. You made quite the recovery." After a shared moment of silence between them, Susan hugged him tightly. "Charlie, your road back to recovery doesn't need to be overwhelming. Find your own new normal. Focus on getting past your grief. There is help out there for you. Find a support group, a therapist, or a qualified professional who can help you navigate through the ups and downs because, believe me, there will be ups and downs." Susan then reached into the pocket of her V-neck scrub top and handed Charlie a piece of paper that contained several names and phones numbers. Before departing his room, she turned around, smiled warmly at Charlie, and said, "Remember, deal with your grief and don't let it hold you hostage. Don't worry so much about rekindling lost friendships or mending past hurts, that will come in time. I am living proof that life after a devastating heartbreak is possible."

With that Susan said her last goodbye and closed the door quietly behind her.

After a brief period of introspection, Charlie started his preparation to leave the hospital. He undressed and tossed his soiled hospital gown into the hamper and headed for the bathroom. He took a very long and warm shower, carefully soaping his still sore and aching body. Once done Charlie toweled off and changed into the same outfit he was rushed to the hospital in: a gray sweatshirt, white t-shirt, and black denims.

Charlie signed out of St. Mary's hospital around 3:30 PM. Reaching the hospital exit, Charlie pushed past the heavy metal doors and gradually climbed down several banks of stairs before descending into the busy city streets. The late afternoon heat accosted him. Streams of perspiration lined Charlie's body before swelling into a river of sweat. Undeterred Charlie slogged through the suffocating heat, jaywalked across a two-lane highway until he reached Parks Road, a small side street adjacent to a large strip mall where swarms of passengers awaited the city bus.

BY NOW CHARLIE WAS PARCHED FROM THE HEAT AND WATER deprivation. When he absentmindedly licked his lips, a habit of his since childhood, he felt the numbing pain of severely chapped lips and tasted the sour mix of blood and sweat. After a while, Charlie forgot his lips were aching. What he needed more than anything was a break from the smothering heat. It was then he noticed a large palm tree a few yards away. Finally, at rest and somewhat cooled down, Charlie inspected his wallet for cash. He was disappointed to only discover a couple of singles and three lousy quarters: a $2.75 take.

As Charlie readied to chuck his wallet away in anger and disappointment, a folded note fell out. Charlie picked up the note from the ground. While inspecting it, five $20 bills spilled out and landed on the ground, barely escaping his grasp. He joyfully collected the $100 and read the accompanying note, which was addressed to him in a beautifully handwritten letter:

Dear Charlie:

By the time you find this note, my pal, you'll be gone and hopefully moving in a positive direction in your life. I've tried not to cry as I write this letter but, I have to confess, I didn't succeed. I will miss you. I'll miss our long talks and the funny stories we shared in our brief time together. You're not like most patients I've treated. You have a soul of gold, and that's unmistakable. You were overall a joy to be around. Anyhow, I thought you could use some help to ease your transition. We all need a helping hand sometimes, so please kindly accept this money as a small token of the confidence I have that you will bounce back stronger than ever. I know I'm not supposed to get personally involved in my patients' lives, but I couldn't help it with you, Charlie. Maybe I'm too much of a softie and stick my nose in business I'm not supposed to, but I did not get into this profession for money or status. I got into it to make a difference. My kids always chastise me about being overly generous with my time and heart. I supposed that's true; however, I would not have it any other way.

Take care of yourself, Charlie.

With warmest regards,
Susan Henderson

AFTER CHARLIE FINISHED READING THE ACCOMPANYING NOTE, feelings of happiness and gratitude sprouted within him. A tear escaped his right eye and gently rolled down his face. He was overwhelmed with appreciation. Susan's benevolent act—her kind and inspiring letter and the generosity of her money—renewed his faith in humanity, further inspiring him to change his dreary circumstances. Charlie thought of how this wonderful angelic woman, a relative stranger, would invest so much in him, whereas a former lover with far greater history, intimacy, and personal stake would treat him so heartlessly, discarding him without so much of an afterthought. The irony of his predicament was exasperating.

With home as his destination, Charlie proceeded to a nearby bus stop. He saw the bus pulling up across the street. He ran for it, against the light, and made it. He made his way pass the crowd of passengers leaving the bus, and got on.

As he pushed his way against the boarding passengers, an angry man turned to him and said, "Who do you think you're pushing here?"

Ignoring him Charlie dropped $1.50 in the money slot and maneuvered past a throng of aimless people. As Charlie continued to make his way to the back of the bus, a man in a seat next to a mother with a young child stared straight ahead with the infinitely tired expression of a late afternoon bus passenger. The mother held her daughter on her lap. The little girl was reading to her mother from a little red children's book.

"That's the problem with young people these days," the angry man continued. "They don't have respect for anyone, especially their elders." The man's chest expanded, and he exhaled nosily. His fiery eyes widened in anger.

Wanting to deescalate the growing tension between the old man and himself, Charlie continued on his path to the back of the bus, navigating through groups of surly faces—the old and young, the skinny and overweight, passengers of varying ages, genders, and ethnicities. Along the way, he observed an older Black woman in an oversized flower dress. She wore brown stockings the color of mocha, and a brown wig that was ill-fitted to her square head. To everyone's consternation, the old lady blew her nose repeatedly into her handkerchief, filling it with piles of snot. And when she coughed, globs of phlegm came out of her mouth. As if making a collective point, several nearby passengers held their hands over their mouths in disgust.

Sitting next to the older Black woman, a graying older White man with a walking cane was in a middle of a monologue, babbling boisterously as he punctured an imaginary balloon with his index finger. He reeked of day-old booze and vile stench. His hair was dirty brown, crudely matted, and draped to his narrow shoulders. Every now and then, the drifter would stand up, say something unintelligible, then sit back down again. The older Black lady seemed unbothered by the man's bizarre behavior, and in fact, rather enjoyed it. She appeared to be the only one.

When the bus driver announced that the Sunset Beach stop was coming up, Charlie made the decision to take a detour from his destination. He was not in a rush to get back to his empty apartment. When the bus arrived at the Sunset Beach stop, he eagerly jumped out of his seat, exited the bus, and walked the short distance to the entrance of the beach.

The day's once bright sky grew dark as radiant sunshine gave way to a breathtaking evening with the silhouette of the sun looming over the Earth. Above white puffy clouds inaugurated the ensemble cast of brilliant shiny stars in the darkening skies. As the ocean's waters slammed against the sea rocks, chipping away at its bedrock, a light, calm breeze swept silently through the night. Except for the battering of the ocean's waters against the rocks, the night was uncannily quiet and still. Nature was at its most tranquil, with all life forms existing harmoniously together. An ideal sanctuary for lost souls, Charlie thought.

For a brief moment, Charlie lingered at the base of the sea. He gazed up at the deserted beach, watching the stars appear and disappear in the darkness of the sky.

He had come to Sunset Beach seeking solitude, clarity, and peace of mind. In this moment in time, human contact was something Charlie was looking to avoid. But life doesn't always succumb to our wishes; and on that fateful day, Charlie's life would change forever.

The miracle began when Charlie noticed the silhouette of a woman sitting a short distance away from him across the sand dunes. Charlie sensed a sadness in the young woman that was familiar to him. Dejected over his own miserable predicament, Charlie was apprehensive about interfering in another person's affairs. But he couldn't stop looking over at the young woman, and after a while, his curiosity got the best of him. He got up from where he was sitting and started heading in her direction. Before long she was in his crosshairs.

"Hello," Charlie said.

Seconds passed, and there was no answer. The woman didn't seem to notice Charlie standing in front of her. During the intermission, the sounds of the ocean waves rocked the silence, and then while still avoiding Charlie's eyes, the young woman began sobbing uncontrollably.

Charlie froze. He didn't know what to do.

After a while, her loud weeping subsided to a soft, gentle sob, and she said, "Why? What did I do to deserve this? How could I let this happen to me?"

Tears flowed down her cheeks, slowly at first. Then in an instant, the tears came bearing down all at once, pouring down her face like an angry river cascading off a steep hill. With the back of her hand, she gently wiped her cheeks. Her gaze finally met Charlie's.

Her beauty was unmistakable. Her eyes were a rich brown color and were shaped like almonds. Her hair, golden brown, was long and fit; each strand of hair seemed independently strong. She had a small mole on her right cheek, and her silky-smooth skin sparkled lustrously under the glowing moonlight.

"What's the matter? "Charlie asked with concern in his voice.

"Nothing, really," she said while wiping away more tears. She stared straight ahead at the darkening skies; her face masked in deep pain. He moved steadily towards her, hoping she would feel comfortable enough to share her troubles with him. He sat next to her in silence for what seemed like an eternity. She finally broke her silence, "Sorry, I don't mean to ignore you. My name is Wanda."

"I'm Charlie." He extended a hand.

When Wanda did not acknowledge his peace offering. He placed his hand back down, feeling slightly self-conscious.

After a while, the quietness between them dissipated, and Wanda blurted, "I hate that man. That son of bitch ruined my life!" New tears formed in Wanda's eyes and gradually trickled down both sides of her face, moistening the bridge of her nose. Charlie reflexively attempted to wipe her face with a tissue he had in his hand, but she quickly pushed his hand away. "What are you doing? Please don't do that. I don't need your pity," said Wanda.

"I am not in the pity business, just trying to offer help. That's all."

"Help? How do you propose to do that? By drying my tears and whispering sweet nothings in my ears while you stalk your prey, readying for the kill? I've read that chapter before."

"I'm sorry," Charlie uttered regrettably. "I suppose your

concerns are well-founded. You don't know me from Adam. But I assure you, I don't have any such intentions."

Wanda exhaled softly. She stared directly into the sky for a brief moment before turning her focus back to Charlie.

"My ex-husband, Chad, was the love of my life. He was my foundation, my rock, the reason for my existence. He was the only person I had ever loved. Our story was full of such promise," Wanda continued. "He was tall, handsome, had a great smile, curious brown eyes, and possessed the swagger of a man who had command of life. I was instantly smitten. We married after three months of intense dating—his idea to do so; I wanted to wait a little longer. The passion between us was surreal. But soon our storybook romance gave way to something more ominous." Wanda broke off, and Charlie thought she was sorting through the terrible moments of her relationship in her mind. "It turned out Chad had another family, a wife and three young kids. Laughable as it may sound, I was prepared to deal with his affair. I rationalized a lot of men have affairs and keep a temptress around for whenever the occasion suited their needs. But Chad's level of deception was beyond the pale, I was crushed!"

"This must be hard for you," Charlie said in a gentle tone. "You do not have to continue if the pain is too much." His eyes held worry for her.

She stood up and walked away from Charlie before circling back to him.

"Sorry," she said, "I lost my cool. I am angry with myself because I should have paid closer attention to the warning signs. In a blinding rage over his betrayal, I threw his clothes and cherished possessions out on the front yard. That same night, Chad came storming into our home; without a word, he barged through our bedroom door and punched me in the face. The impact of his blow was ear splitting. I hit the hardwood floor with a thud. I was concussed. When I finally came to, I was in unimaginable agony. I somehow managed to pick up the phone and dialed 911 for help. My life after that horrific experience was never the same. I spent a year in therapy and in a domestic abuse group exchanging horror stories with like-minded survivors. For a while, I didn't know how I was going to pick up the pieces or even get back to a semblance of normalcy. Through physical therapy and counseling, I reconstructed parts of me that were broken, but it wasn't until much later in the healing process I began to forgive myself. I had also resolved that I was not going to be the victim in this tragedy, and accepted that Chad's behavior wasn't my fault. But from time to time, I still carry around some of the baggage from that horrific experience." While Wanda rummaged through her emotions, Charlie remained quiet.

Wanda broke the silence, "I sometimes still think of Chad as that gentle, caring man. Is something wrong with me?"

"No, there isn't," Charlie said. "Those good parts were there."

"Although the incident happened years ago, coming to Sunset Beach every year has been a spiritual cleansing of a sort," Wanda said with a sigh of relief. "It has allowed me to chip away at the pain and sorrow and has released some of the past hurts from my heart. Some years I feel completely at peace. Other times, I'm like the way I am today. I am amazed at how far I've come but still remain surprised to know I still harbor such strong sentiments for him years later."

"Love is a very complex and an unpredictable emotion. You can't always control how it behaves," Charlie said with compassion in his voice, remembering his own heartbreak.

They gazed into each other's eyes and something clicked, but the weight of their past hurts left Charlie and Wanda too vulnerable, and they quickly averted their eyes.

Wanda stood up. "Charlie, thank you for listening to me," she said. "Talking to you about my plight has been be so cathartic."

"You're welcome," Charlie said.

Then Wanda asked, "What is your story, Charlie? What brings you to Sunset Beach?"

Charlie hesitated, but something in him felt comfortable enough with Wanda to let his guard down. After all she had trusted him enough to share her story. Charlie proceeded to recount his relationship with Sherrie, her duplicity, their break-up, his attempted suicide, his stay at St. Mary's hospital, Susan Henderson's warmth towards him…all the things that led to his coming to Sunset Beach for solace.

When Charlie was done, Wanda looked over at him with concern in her eyes and said, "I'm sorry you went through that, Charlie."

"Thank you, Wanda. I'm sorry you went through what you did also."

Both Charlie and Wanda sat at the beach a little while longer, looking at the half-moon in the night's sky and twinkling stars. Neither wanted the night to end. They wanted to ask for each other's phone number, but somehow felt that would ruin the moment. As the night sky grew darker, Wanda and Charlie went their separate ways, a little lighter and more hopeful about their futures.

At half past 8:00 P.M., Charlie arrived at his apartment. To his pleasant surprise, his neighbor Raymond had cleaned his place and stocked his refrigerator with a few items. He picked up the phone and called Raymond to thank him, but there was no answer. He left a message of appreciation for Raymond, thanking him for everything he did for him. Charlie then headed to his bedroom to get ready for bed, removed his dirty clothes, and put on a pair of clean pajamas. He attempted to sleep, but he couldn't get Wanda out of his thoughts.

He wondered whether she arrived home safely. He had a strong desire to take care of her, to take away the pain she was feeling. After a couple of hours, Charlie finally succumbed to his tiredness and fell asleep.

He awoke the next morning with Wanda on his mind. He wondered if he should go to Sunset Beach, hoping maybe she would be there. He dismissed the idea as soon as it came into his thoughts, convincing himself it was a bad idea...only to later decide he would take a leap of faith.

Charlie returned to Sunset Beach a few minutes before sunset. He walked quietly along the ocean, feeling the full force of the chilled waters as they splashed against his feet, and suddenly he saw Wanda approaching him. He couldn't believe his eyes. Giddy with excitement, he quickened his pace to meet her.

"Hello, Charlie," she said with a smile on her face.

"Hello, Wanda," he responded in kind.

And with that, Charlie and Wanda opened their hearts to the possibility of a more promising future ahead.